59372084547101   WDWD

D0457716

W I T H D R A W N

WORN, SOILED, OBSOLETE

ONE

CROW

ALONE

ONE CROW ALONE

S. D. CROCKETT

FEIWEL AND FRIENDS

NEW YORK

A FEIWEL AND FRIENDS BOOK
An Imprint of Macmillan

ONE CROW ALONE. Copyright © 2013 by S. D. Crockett. All rights reserved. Printed in the United States of America by R. R. Donnelley & Sons Company, Harrisonburg, Virginia. For information, address Feiwel and Friends, 175 Fifth Avenue, New York, N.Y. 10010.

Feiwel and Friends books may be purchased for business or promotional use. For information on bulk purchases, please contact the Macmillan Corporate and Premium Sales Department at (800) 221-7945 x5442 or by e-mail at specialmarkets@macmillan.com.

Library of Congress Cataloging-in-Publication Data Available

ISBN: 978-1-250-02425-1 (hardcover) / 978-1-4668-4844-3 (ebook)

Book design by Barbara Grzeslo

Feiwel and Friends logo designed by Filomena Tuosto

First Edition: 2013

10 9 8 7 6 5 4 3 2 1

macteenbooks.com

For my mother

*The Crow is a bird of long life, and diviners tell
that she taketh heed of spyings and awaitings,
and teacheth and sheweth ways, and warneth
what shall fall.*

*—But it is full unlawful to believe that
God sheweth His privy counsel to Crows.*

—Bartholomaeus Anglicus,
De proprietatibus rerum, thirteenth century

High on a wave-battered cliff is a simple cottage built of stone. It clings to the black rocks above a churning, wide-gray sea. Smoke from a narrow chimney is beaten horizontal by the wind.

Inside the cottage a girl tends the fire.

But her baby will not sleep.

• • •

"Do stop crying," the girl said. "It's only September and not too cold." She picked the child up and held it in her arms. "I'll tell you a story if you're quiet for a second." She went to the window. "Look. There's Da coming up the path."

It wasn't long before a young man stooped in out of the wind and laid a fish on the table. "I ain't gonna go out no more in that wind, Mary," he said, pulling a chair up to the fire. And his dog—which had slunk in from outside—lay down at his feet like sensible dogs do.

"The baby been quiet?" he asked.

"No," said the girl.

"Ain't got no rope trailing behind it," he said. "Nothing tying it to before. No wonder it blubs all day long."

"I'm going to tell her a story to keep her quiet."

"Bout what?"

"About Magda."

"What do you know about Magda? I can tell the kid some things."

"I know what Da told me," Mary said. "But I can't do it with you sticking your nose in."

Willo sat back and took off his boots. "I won't stick my nose in—even if you do get it all wrong. I'll just sit here quiet and listen. Ain't heard a good Tell in a while."

So Mary took a place by the fire. And comforting the baby in her arms she closed her eyes—and began:

WINTER

Once upon a time ... When Crow again came to walk about on this earth amongst men, and a shadow came to fall over the land, there lived a poor woman and her granddaughter—hard by a Great Forest.

I

Of course there were summers.

But not then.

January. When the low wooden cottages with their graying boards and damp-swollen shutters and rickety porches on wide-planked verandas sat buried in whiteness at the foot of the hill.

When stacks of split logs were piled under snow-heavy roofs and animals shifted in dung-smelling barns and dogs forever tied bored on heavy chains.

It begins here.

With a priest.

Pulling his collar close as he limped along the snow-covered track that ran through a village called Morochov.

• • •

Kraa! Kraa!

How will it end?

With children digging graves.

Kraa! Kraa!

• • •

The priest grabbed a burnt coal from the cinder-strewn path: *Bugger off!* He threw it at the cawing crow. *Aagh*—He gripped his aching knee. Limped toward a small cottage, the hem of his coat growing damp as it skimmed the banks of shoveled snow.

He peered over the broken stick fence bounding the garden. Just a bloom of smoke hovered about the roof of the house. Icicles hung under the eaves—the faded shutters were closed tight against the cold.

Inside the cottage an old woman was dying. The priest had come to hear her last words.

How long since anyone official has been? he thought. *There has been no one since the power lines came down.*

As his hand rested on the gate, he caught a movement in the garden. In the deep snow under the bare apple trees a girl hacked at a half-dug grave. He could see her belted coat straining as she lifted the heavy pick above her head.

Clud clud clud. The fresh earth piled black against the snow.

"Magda," the priest called out.

The girl stopped her cludding and came over. Breathless, she leaned the handle of the pick against the gatepost. Sweat dampened the fur under the rim of her hat. She led him silently up the icy steps of the veranda. Stamping snow in the small, open porch, they took off their boots and went into the house.

In the darkened bedroom, her grandmother lay on a high iron bed like a statue under the heavy covers. The old woman's lips were dry and her breathing was slow and her skin had begun to tighten and sink onto the bones of her cheeks.

The priest pulled up a chair and the old woman opened her eyes.

"I am here," she said.

"Babula—" Magda held the pale fingers and kissed her grand-mother's face and offered a cloth. The priest wiped his hands, heard the old woman's whispered secrets, and late in the after-noon, after anointing her, he closed her eyes for the last time.

"By the sacred mysteries of man's redemption, may Almighty God remit to you all penalties of the present life and of the life to come. May He open to you the gates of paradise and lead you to joys everlasting."

Magda, bowing her head, said.

"Amen."

• • •

Shh! The nuts and bolts of dying are nothing more than that. Sen-timent, like the big bottle of iodine that stings in a wound, was locked away in the cupboard.

• • •

So the priest said his words, drained the cup of vodka set out on the table, and fetched the Dudek brothers from the neighboring house. The snow that fell from their boots melted on the floor-boards. They helped lay the body in the open coffin between the chairs in the kitchen, their damp soles shuffling on the bare scrubbed planks.

They didn't talk much.

Looked at Magda as she lifted the hatch in the floor and stepped down into the cellar.

"Thank you," Magda said, handing them a bag of potatoes. The priest too.

"She was a good woman," said Aleksy.

"What're you going to do now?" asked his brother Brunon, staring at the hatch in the floor.

"I don't know," Magda replied.

"I mean—with all them potatoes?"

Magda stepped back onto the closed cellar hatch. They left.

But when they had gone the priest asked the same thing.

"What are you going to do, Magda?"

"What do you mean?" she said, washing his cup at the sink.

"You can't stay here on your own now your grandmother is dead. Bogdan Stopko is growing lonely. You know he has two fields—a tractor and a pony. You're sixteen, aren't you? He is not a bad man. And good men don't grow like brambles."

Magda turned from the sink. "You're saying he's rich—not good."

"He's rich in those things which I say. That's half and half of his being good."

She dried her hands. "I don't know. I don't know what I should do. It's the middle of winter. I haven't heard from Mama since the power lines came down."

"Then maybe you should go to London. You can't stay here alone forever—"

"London? How will I get to London?" Magda hung the cloth, bent down, and checked the stove; she threw in a few logs and looked up at him. "How will I do that?"

Having no answer, the priest picked his hat up off the table and left. It was growing dark outside.

His own fire needed tending.

2

In the darkness under the trees, three trucks came to a stop. Engines ticked over in the freezing night air. Men jumped out onto the hardpack of the road. Moved like shadows against the snow.

Under the higgledy roofs of the wooden houses scattered along the valley, everyone slept.

But Magda heard a dog. Bogdan Stopko's dog. Why did it bark in the middle of the night?

She sat up. Lit the candle by her bed. The ice on the inside of the window was as thick as glass. She rubbed her finger on it. Peered through the cracks in the shutter.

Against the pale snow she could see the silhouette of the fence and the lumpen, snow-topped shadow of Bogdan Stopko's house off on the other side of the street.

The dog stopped barking.

She should be praying over Babula's coffin, not sleeping. But she had been so tired.

She rubbed at the glass again.

Then she saw the men. Two figures. Coming along the fence. She pulled back.

If the marauders come stealing, you must hide, Magda.

Quickly. A fumble for matches. Out of bed.

With a small candle trailing shadows behind her in the dark, she tiptoed across the bare wooden boards, stopped, and crossed herself over the body of her grandmother.

Lifting the hatch in the floor, she looked down into the dark cellar. *Before you have stepped into the cellar with Grandmother, your own Babula, clucking like a hen, passing down the sacks of potatoes or calling for you to fetch the salted butter—Close the barrel tight, Magda!*

• • •

There was a scraping on the porch. Magda blew out the fluttering candle and it was as dark as Hell. Her feet in woolen stockings fumbled for the cellar steps. Heart pounding, she felt her way down and pulled the hatch over her head.

If you had a light, it would warm your fingers and you would see the jars along the beam. Pickled mushroom and cabbage and wild strawberries.

But the darkness was a shelter and she crept further into it. Listening. Waiting. Felt the cold, packed earth under her feet. Like a mouse, she tried to make herself small among the musty sacks of potatoes.

But you are not a mouse and cannot hide like one, and if they come down here they will find you. Maybe they will only take food.

There were footsteps on the wooden boards of the porch. Stomping footsteps. The rattling of the flimsy door. Bashing on it.

"Open up! Open up in there!"

Her hands were shaking. She pushed her face into the sacks and breathed in the smell of the earth.

If you smell the earth, then you will remember the things that are good and not the footsteps.

Smells that conjure so much in an instant: Babula is in this smell. Mama, she is here too, helping Babula lift potatoes from the dark soil. Mama, bringing money and soap and sweets from London. Always telling Babula: *You have no need, old Mother, I send money so you do not have to lift your potatoes every year. Sit back, eat cherries. Magda is here to look after you.*

But when Mama has gone, Babula leans close and whispers: *I lift these potatoes because I have been hungry before and the potatoes kept me alive then. Remember that. But you*—she puts her hand out, bent like an old root and pale. *But you, little Magda—why do you stay? Go. Do not stay here with the old ones. Keep learning to speak your English. One day I will be gone.*

And if you cry, and tell her that you do not really know your mother—that you will never leave the village, Babula will tell you a story.

These are real stories, Magda, she says. *Because the television is no good when you have no electricity. And we've had no power all winter. No power, no television, no telephone.*

The old stories that Babula tells with her soft hand on your face. They are good; they do not need electricity to hear them.

The story of Crow is coming right out of the sacks of potatoes. "OPEN UP!"

The men outside are shouting and bashing.

Thump. Thump. Walls rattling.

. . .

I'll tell you the story of Girl and Crow, Babula begins with a warning look. *Oh, the girl was poor—but she was good. And the crow was a beast of a crow. It had dark eyes, Magda,* Babula whispers. *Dark eyes. In its dark head.*

. . .

"Open up, I tell you!" come the voices, loud and impatient.

. . .

It was winter. And the girl went to the forest for firewood—as she must. Her feet were cold and her hands were cold. And when she had gone some way she found Crow in the thicket.

. . .

"Goddamn this cold. Open up!"

. . .

*Crow was eating—*Babula will make an ugly face—*like this ... with its dirty claws bent over a dead wolf. Ripping the bloody entrails with its strong beak. The girl saw that it was just hungry, and she felt sorry and held out the last piece of cake from her pocket. It was a good cake—*

. . .

"Open up!"

There was a splintering of wood.

And the footsteps were inside the house. Right above Magda's head.

She heard the striking of a match. Something fell on the floor.

"Use the bloody torch."

The footsteps moved across the room. Light fell between the floorboards above her.

"Tomasz! Here."

They had found the coffin.

Magda felt the beating of the blood in her throat. She clamped her fingers into her hand so hard it hurt. *Please, God, make the men go away.*

"They're dropping like flies out here," said the voice.

"No wonder in this cold."

"Look at the old woman. These village people. Their old ways. They should be left out here to die in peace. What good will it do taking them away?"

"Come on. I'm not carrying out a stiff."

There was a shuffling on the boards. The strangers tramped about the cottage, heavy footfalls in the small room beside the kitchen.

"Nothing here."

Magda heard the broken door scraping on the floor overhead.

And then she was alone.

But she didn't move from the corner of the cellar. Just drew up her feet and pulled the old sacks over her body.

You prayed to God, she thought.

And He made the men go away.

3

Lifting the hatch, barely able to feel her fingers, Magda stuck her head up into the kitchen. An icy wind gusted through the broken door. A thin drift of snow had blown in across the floor.

She heard a cockerel crowing. It was far off—muffled by the shuttered windows. Morning had come. There was no sound except that cockerel.

You'd think the villagers would be out in a gaggle on the street after marauders had been stealing around in the night.

But there was nothing. Just a great silence.

The coffin lay untouched. Babula's face staring at the ceiling with closed, sunken eyes.

Magda went to the bedroom. Everything was untouched: the blankets thrown back as she had left them in the middle of the night.

She took her sweater from the chair. Pulled it over her frozen arms, rolled on thick woolen tights, stuck her legs fast into her trousers.

The oven was growing cold. Just a few smoldering embers left. She lit a candle and took the pot of kasha from the bottom oven where it had been sitting all night. She sat on the stool and gulped it down. It warmed her guts.

You have to be strong. You have to get out there and see what has happened.

She took a pair of gloves, stiff and dry, from the peg above the stove. The broken front door scraped noisily as she wrenched it over the floorboards. The Stopko dog heard the noise. It began to bark. Loudly. Insistently.

Magda looked down the street. The snow was falling thick and heavy. An occasional gust of wind blew it up in clouds around the house, with the smell of cold spiking the blustery air and the drifts growing deeper.

But there was nothing. No one. No sound coming from any of the houses.

The dog continued barking.

You have to go and see what has happened.

Magda came down the steps from the porch, her boots creaking on the newly fallen snow. The wind stung her cheeks and she pulled her hat low and made her way along the track toward the Dudeks' house.

There was no smoke coming from the chimney. She climbed the steps of the long wooden veranda under the frozen eaves.

She knocked on the door.

She knocked again.

A crow cawed and flapped from the top of a tree, dislodging a clump of snow. It swept down behind Stopko's barn far off on the other side of the street.

On a clear day, you could have seen the mountains, and the dark trees of the forest on the slopes not far behind the village.

Now everything was made hazy by the blizzard. The dog barked again.

She felt a sweat under her clothing. Turned the handle of the Dudeks' door. Pushed it open.

"Hello? Brunon? Aleksy?"

The kitchen held the remains of warmth.

"Brunon? Aleksy? It is only me, Magda."

But there was no answer.

· · ·

She made her way to the next cottage, up to Kowalski's porch. Opened the door. Nothing.

Her pace quickened.

Magda left Stopko's door until the last. It was a hope. If Stopko had disappeared, then there was trouble that wasn't going to go away: You don't just turn up and drag Bogdan Stopko out of his warm bed in the middle of the night without a fight.

But she knew as she turned the handle.

His kitchen would be as empty as the others.

· · ·

The village was deserted.

· · ·

Just that dog.

"Stop your barking, Azor!" And when she rounded the side of the house to his kennel the dog did stop barking. He wagged his tail and grimaced with his teeth at the same time.

He was a big white sheepdog, tied on a chain all winter. But he didn't try to bite, seemed pleased to see her, so she untied his collar and set him loose.

The dog shook himself hard. Then came leaping and jumping at her as she made her way to the long barn back behind the sticks of the hazel copse. He cocked his leg against a tree, yellowing a hole in the snow.

"Azor!"

The dog bounded over, up to his chest in the drifts. Magda pulled open the doors of the barn. The smell of hay and animal came rich from inside.

There in the stall was Stopko's pony, picking at forgotten wisps of hay on the ground. It whinnied when she came in. She threw a bundle of hay into the rack, then went outside and hauled a bucket of water from the well. Leaning over the bitten wooden rail of the stall, she filled the stone trough and the pony drank, long and grateful.

Magda sat down on the log pile. Her head sank onto her hands. *You are alone. And you have no idea why. Or how.*

A startled cat hissed from the top of a haystack, its back arched like a briar. The dog barked loudly, throwing himself back on his haunches. The pony started at the commotion, flinging its head up from the hay. Dog gave up, sniffed along the haystack. Came over and stuck his cold nose under Magda's hair. Sparrows flitted in the beams. *Look at the birds of the air; they do not sow, or reap, or gather into barns.*

She pushed the dog away.

You must get back and light the stove.

• • •

There was worse at home. Babula in her coffin. Heavy as lead. No Dudek brothers to help carry her out now. There was just a cellar full of potatoes, a pony—and Stopko's dog.

In some ways it was better that Babula wasn't alive to witness such a morning.

The stove slowly broke into life. Magda regarded the flames with an unfocused gaze and fed sticks through the heavy iron door.

The dog curled up underneath the porch, biting at his tail. Then thought better of such wasted freedom and snuffled off along the drifts.

Magda managed to fix up the broken door so that it closed, and the stove slowly seeped a sort of warmth into the room. She lit a candle and sat beside the coffin.

They have all gone, Babula. Men came in the night. I heard them. They broke the door.

But Babula could not help her.

And Magda pulled the sheet over the old woman's face and turned back to the fire.

Why had they taken the villagers? *All of them.*

Trouble had happened in the village of Zborov last winter. The shepherds told Stopko: "Strangers have been. They came and stole our food, Pan Stopko. What should we do?" Old guns were brought out and hidden under beds by even older men. But in Zborov the strangers had only taken chickens and cheese. They had been hungry marauders from the town, desperate during the long cold winter. Only a few men standing firm over their cellars were hurt. No one taken away. Not like this.

And you heard other news when Bogdan Stopko came back from the market, counting out a wad of zloty with his big, hard hands. "It is snowing in Rome. In Paris. In London. Snowing everywhere! Everyone is hungry. But our mutton and honey are fetching high prices! Keep singing, boys!"

Stopko had even bought a radio.

"Made in China, my friends!"

The men listened to the music crackling out of it. Brunon Dudek, kicking his heels up in the sawdust, a bottle of vodka splashing in his hand, singing badly: "But if you will not drink up, whoever sticks two to it, lupu cupu, cupu lupu, whoever sticks two to it!"

And Babula tutting over a stirred pot. "Our luck is another's misfortune, Magda."

But she had been happy enough with their share of the money.

• • •

Outside, that wretched dog was barking again. Magda got up from her chair beside the coffin. Peered out into the blizzard. The bad day was slipping away. But the dog was only chasing a whirlwind of snow.

You must put Babula in the ground.

Magda took the narrow wooden lid leaning against the wall and placed it on the coffin. She hammered the nails in with a shoe.

Where are you all? Where have you gone?

Soon the dark would fall.

And, like wolves, the spirits of the unburied dead would creep out of the forest, crawl along the frozen river, up the banks to the house, slither through cracks in the door and come creaking over the boards.

Maybe the candle will gutter. And blow out. And it will be the dead of night.

In the dark you will be alone.

And the spirits will *tap tap tap* to wake dead Babula. And her old bent hands will scratch at the coffin lid. *You nailed me in with your shoe, wicked girl!* And the dirty long fingernails of the spirits from the forest will prise the lid open, laughing. *You didn't bury her! You didn't bury her!* They will scratch and rattle, and you will be lying in your bed shaking. In the dark. Because there is no weight of earth covering her. No. You must get her in the ground before nightfall.

. . .

Magda lifted the foot of the coffin, she kicked the chair to one side and rested it heavily on the floor—then did the same with the other end.

Grasping the coffin with both hands, she pulled it across the floor. The rails grated, catching on nail heads and gouging tracks in the floorboards. She kicked the front door open with her foot. It was snowing heavily outside. The wind battered like a shovel, slapping the hair across her face. Then she had it through the door. Out on the porch, the coffin hanging over the step with the full weight of the body inside it weighing on her arms.

The dog appeared at the gate.

She hauled the coffin down the steps. *Cadunk.* She felt the boards sag. She stepped back. The path was icy. She squared her feet and pulled again.

Down came the coffin. *Bump, bump, bump.* Thumping to the bottom of the steps. The body inside it slumping toward her as she fell.

The dog barked.

"Go away!" she shouted.

He slunk backward.

She untangled herself, kneeling in the maelstrom of snow-flakes, rubbing her bruised knee. She put out a hand, turning her mouth from the freezing drafts of wind. "Azor—I didn't mean it. Come, I won't hurt."

Her head sank down onto the rough boards. "Babula," she whispered into them. "Babula, give me strength. I am alone. Try not to be so heavy."

The dog sat a little way off, and Magda put her hands under the coffin once more and began dragging it across the snow. She stopped to catch her breath and looked up at the deserted houses, the rim of trees dark on the hill behind the village. Hadn't she heard Kowalski say that wolves had been seen at the forest edge?

The dog pricked his ears. If she let herself, Magda might have thought he was listening for them. But Kowalski was a worrier: his chickens always egg-bound, his potatoes blighted, his cellar damper than anyone else's. Wolves indeed. Had anyone even heard them?

With a final heave, she pushed the coffin into the shallow grave. With a dull thump, it slid down on its side, sending up a puff of snow. But the lid held. With the last of her strength, Magda hacked the frozen pile of earth down onto it.

She said the prayers she thought the priest would have spoken.

But everything was wrong.

Even now it did not seem possible that Babula wasn't stirring a pot in the kitchen. Magda made her way, trembling, with sad steps back to the house. "Azor. Come."

He looked up. "Come," she repeated quietly.

Slowly the dog crept up the steps.

"Come on. Come inside."

He put his paw tentatively over the threshold. She dragged him by the scruff of his neck. Pushed the door shut. Locked it. Breathed a little easier.

"You can eat kasha, dog." She took an enameled basin from above the stove and ladled the remains of the morning's porridge into it.

"See. You are the man of the house." She placed the bowl on the floor. "Fleas or no fleas, you have to look after me now."

It felt better not to be alone.

Mama said that in England people had dogs living in their houses. They let them sleep on the bed. On the bed, Azor! They had coats for their dogs. And chocolate. There were *whole shops* selling coats and chocolates for dogs.

Azor wolfed down the kasha, sniffed about, slumped panting beside the door and closed his eyes.

Magda piled fresh wood into the stove. Pulled off her boots.

At least Babula had died peacefully. Kowalski's wife making the soup in the last days, and holding Magda's hand. What more could she do? Magda had no way of contacting her mother even. No way to tell her: Babula is dead. I'm alone, Mama—

And now what? Wait?

Babula would have said, "If you have no answer, then make no decision. Sleep on it. When everything stops making sense, then sense is all that's left. It is better, Magda, that you suffer for doing what is right, than for doing what is wrong."

A wind rattled the shutters.

In the fading afternoon light, Magda sat by the stove. When her eyes could stay open no longer, she crawled into bed, pulled the cover over her head, and listened to her own breath against the pillow.

There is no use in crying. Death comes to everyone. It is just the way. And whatever has happened in the village has happened. There must be some explanation. Tomorrow, maybe tomorrow, the storm will break. Tomorrow you will have to think what to do. But now there is no better thing to do than sleep.

She kicked the blankets up around her cold feet, drew them in, and turned to the wall.

In that terrible dark loneliness she was thankful at least for the dog guarding the door.

4

For a moment, as she woke, Magda forgot.

For a moment, everything was as it should be.

But the moment was gone with the opening of her eyes. She pushed the blankets back and got up.

In the kitchen, the dog beat his tail on the floor a few times. She caught sight of herself in the mirror above the dresser. Tugged at her hair. Stoked up the stove.

What will you do?

Babula would have prayed. But it would be better to go and fetch water from the well. There was the pony to feed.

She poured the last of the water from the pitcher into a pan of oats.

• • •

Stopko's radio!

• • •

Magda flung the pan onto the stove. Threw on her coat and boots.

"Azor. The radio!"

Stopko's Chinese radio. Maybe there was life in the battery.

The dog bounded after her through the snow. She ran across the street and jumped the steps to his door.

The door creaked open. The house was already cold with no

fire to warm it. The television sat on top of an old cupboard. Magda pulled open the drawers: neatly stacked DVDs and a pile of faded newspapers lay inside. She went to the bedroom. Stopko's bed was unmade. As if he had just got out of it. The room still smelled stale. And there. On the table beside the bed was an empty bottle of vodka. And the radio. She grabbed it.

Back at home, Magda put the radio on the table. Her hands were shaking.

She switched it on.

Nothing.

She took the batteries out. Rubbed the greening connections inside the compartment. Placed the batteries in the lowest oven of the stove—she had seen Stopko doing it—ten minutes maybe, but not too hot, so she left the oven door open.

Please, God, make them work.

She inserted the batteries back into the radio.

Switched it on.

The radio crackled into life. *Krrrrghhhh. Krck. Kurrr.*

The antenna. She pulled it up, turned the dial.

Kughrrr. Krck. A voice faded in across the airwaves.

"—ee evacuated to the nearest city. Government forces will reach you soon. Wait in your houses. I repeat, a State of Emergency has been declared. Bring only what you can carry. *Krck. Krr.* Government forces will be with you soon. Citizens of Malpolskie District. This is your governor speaking. All villages will be evacuated to the . . ."

The batteries died and the voice faded away.

· · ·

Magda's heart felt as if it had fallen to the ground and rolled away like a stone. *The men who came were not coming to steal—they were coming to evacuate the village. And you hid. Hid in the cellar.*

Why had no one noticed she was missing? But then, of course, it would have been dark. Mayhem, villagers not wanting to go, animals dragged out of barns, old women crying, Stopko shouting.

But why had the men come? What was the emergency? What terrible thing had happened?

Maybe it was the snow. The power lines had come down and no one had mended them, it was true. The villagers had talked. But they didn't question after a week or two. What could you do anyway? they said. It makes no difference to us. We have our pickled cabbage and apples in the attic. Summer will come.

You will have to go to the village of Mokre. Someone must be there. Someone who will know . . .

Magda did not know what else she could do.

A log cracked in the stove. She pressed the buttons, but the radio would not come to life again.

She took a piece of paper and laid it on the table.

Wrote a message and weighted it down with a cup:

I have been left behind in the village. The weather is very bad. I will take Bogdan Stopko's pony and try to reach the village of Mokre. If there is no one there, I will go to the road and try to find the others.

God help me.

Magda Krol

10 January 2039

She looked about the kitchen. On a high shelf by the window was Babula's small Bible. She took it down. Old and worn, the Bible was inscribed on the first page:

Agnieszka Maria Krol

1958

And written below that in a child's hand:

In the fear of the Lord is strong confidence and his children shall have a place of refuge.

Magda took out the faded piece of paper with her mother's address and telephone number on it, folded it very carefully, and put it in her shirt pocket. Then laid the Bible back on the shelf.

She took a deep breath and looked about at the familiar walls. The clock ticked loudly on the shelf.

There will be no one to wind it until you return.

She wrapped some bread and the remains of a ham, filled a bag with oats, took a sliver of soap from the sink, then rolled the blankets from the bed and tied them to her bag.

At the door she turned, glanced one more time at the scrubbed wooden table and worn floorboards, at the mugs hanging above the sink and the photographs on the wall.

She pulled her hat tight over her ears. What use was there in crying over yesterday's burnt kasha?

• • •

The dog was sitting by Stopko's fence.

"There is nothing for you where I'm going, Azor. No kasha, no meat. Nothing."

But there was nothing for him in the village either and he stuck to her ankles like a tick.

The pony was well fed, a little round in the hindquarters even, his dun-colored winter coat dirty and unbrushed. He hung his head low as Magda threw the rope over his neck, a dark wiry mane falling this way and that. She grabbed a handful and scrambled onto his back. The pony flattened his ears and twisted his neck and nipped at her leg. She swiped it away and buried her gloved hands in the tangled mane and kicked him on into the weather, with Azor trotting at their heels, down to the icy riverbank and the blizzard still graying the big, wide sky.

It was no day to make a journey.

• • •

A mile or so later the pony snorted his way up the bank between the low, shuttered houses of Mokre.

Every house was shut and empty. No need to knock on doors. There was no smoke, no nothing.

28

She turned her head, looked out at the snow-covered hills all about, the dark of the forest traced on the skyline, the distant mountains looming over the empty village with intent.

You are just a speck on this earth. Who will care if you sink in the snow and are covered? These mountains won't care.

The wind gusted, unrelenting. Maybe she should take the low road to Karlikov. There might be other people there. Just maybe.

She clucked at the pony and retraced her steps down the slope, the dog following close.

When she had gone as far as she could along the riverbank, she headed up to where the road should have been. She stared at the deep white all about. Slid off the pony's back. A freezing wall of wind took away her breath.

If you had been beating against the winds high above, you would have seen the tiny figures shrouded in the storm, bending against the weather: struggling and sinking and sweating and freezing. Drowning in the snow like ants in a puddle. And Magda, shielding her face, breathing hard against the upturned collar of her coat, looked up at the hillside—still visible through a haze of snowflakes—and managed to cajole the sweating pony; up to that bush there, the top of a rock jutting through the snow, a little higher to that sheltering tree. Up, up, up. Out of the drifts. It had been madness to try to take the low road. If she could just reach that firmer ground higher up, then she would be able to get to the shelter of the forest—and over the hill to Karlikov before nightfall. She pushed Kowalski's tales of wolves to the back of her mind.

. . .

At last she came in among the trees.

Two jays set up a racketing clatter high in the branches. The blizzard lashed the treetops, swaying and creaking overhead, but there was a kind of calm on the forest floor, and she stopped for a moment to catch her breath.

The weather is impossible. You should have waited. Should have sat by the stove with a plate of hot food for a day more.

The dog wagged its snow-crusted tail. Well, there was no understanding dogs.

And if she found the foresters' track she was certain she could reach the northern edge of the forest before nightfall. *Wolves indeed, you foolish girl!* She picked her way under the sheltering boughs with growing confidence.

But she hadn't realized how long it had taken her to climb the hill. By four o'clock the winter sun began to drop below the horizon. The gray sky, shrouded already by the forest, grew dim and bleak.

Yes, dusk came quickly. All of a sudden she could barely see the trees looming around her.

"Azor." She wanted him close.

She tried to calm her rapidly beating heart. *It's not far to Karlikov. It is only the sinking sun that has changed everything. The world hasn't changed. It hasn't disappeared. It is only the coming nighttime.*

But she found that the heartbeat of the dusk-fallen forest was stronger than her prayers. The dark dropped like a curtain. There was something in it that gripped her innards. The twisted tree trunks seemed grim specters. Reaching out from dusky shadows. There was no safe corner to put her back against.

"Aagh!" Her shins hit a fallen branch. She stumbled down onto her knees. Up ahead was a bright swathe under the trees. She clutched the pony's rope and pulled herself up. The night sky rushed with unseen clouds and the shuttered moon appeared briefly from behind them and lit the edge of a clearing. She stepped out with loud breaths, her boots crunching across a glowing ribbon of open snow.

On the other side of the track was something square and solid in the gloom.

A twig snapped.

She stopped as still as a post. The wind rattled the treetops.

It was a broken-down foresters' hut, the door hanging open—weathered boards roughly nailed to the walls under a snowy tin roof. A fallen branch lay over one side.

Magda lashed the pony to a tree and pulled at the stiff wooden door, leapt back in fright as a clutch of twigs fell at her feet.

The hut smelled damp. It smelled of earth. She peeled the rucksack from her shoulder and dug about for the matches. Struck one.

The interior appeared in its guttering flame. Dusty cobwebs sagged in the corners. Ivy had grown in through the walls—snaking up through gaps in the boards. Along the back wall was a low bench with dead leaves heaped in mounds on top of it, an untidy pile of sticks beneath, and a small flat-topped stove rusting in the corner.

Kneeling down, Magda opened the stove and piled a handful

of dry leaves on top of the congealed char inside it, and shielding the match with her hand she lit the tinder.

Soon the fire was burning strong. She crouched down with her arms around her knees. Tried to forget the fears hammering inside her head—*claang claang claang*—like a blacksmith at his anvil. Struggling to make sense of it all somehow.

It was true the villagers had begun to talk. Even Babula. *These are the hardest winters I have ever seen, Magda. And now too in Paris? In Rome? Those are places! God help your mother. Maybe it is bad in London too?—You must call her.*

Standing by Stopko's door holding out a bowl of strawberries. "I want to use your telephone to phone my mother. Grandmother has sent these."

"Pretty Magda, come and sit on my knee!" Stopko had slurred.

At least thirty and no wife. Still drunk from his success at the market. Slumped by the dirty stove. With his boots on!

"Nearly sixteen now, aren't you," he said, waving his hand clumsily.

But he let her edge around him like a frightened dog. And she called the number written on the faded piece of paper—

Magda loosened her boots, thought about that last call. Standing in Bogdan Stopko's house, turned to the wall, speaking to her mother. When she had finished, Stopko wanted to know everything.

"What news, young Magda? Come on. I won't bite. I let you make the call. The expensive call to England. And you can keep the strawberries. Eat them and think of me when you do, ha!"

But the news—

"She says things are bad."

"She lost her job? She should be looking after her own child. Here. Where she belongs."

"No. Not that. She says it is very cold. And food has become too expensive. Even the English are hungry."

"Keep digging, boys!" Stopko burped.

"She wants to come back. But there are no buses home. Nothing is working. She says it is turning ugly."

• • •

How long ago had she made that call? Months? Magda's head sank to her knees. It had been the last time she had spoken to her mother. Before, everything had had its place, Babula and Magda quiet together like peas in a pod. Mama sending money from London. Writing letters—telling the story about how they would all be together one day: Magda, Mama, and Babula, an apartment in town—she wrote about her job and the people she worked for, the children she looked after, the shops where you could buy the clothes and shoes and sweets that spilled out of her bag as soon as she walked up the steps of the porch, tired from the long bus journey from England.

I am saving, saving for your future, my little Magda.

But then there is the scene before Mama leaves for the bus back to London, the scene where the bedroom door is closed. Babula sending you outside even though you are too old to play.

Even outside you can hear Mama crying through the shutters.

And you think to yourself, I will never leave Morochov, or Babula. However many things she brings in her bag.

And now you must find Mama and tell her that Babula—your own Babula—is dead.

Magda put another stick on the fire. She thought of the pony out in the cold.

There is no time to crowd your head with tomorrow's problems.

She took a blanket and went out to lay it over the pony's back. But out in the forest the darkness overwhelmed her, and she fled back to the safety of the fire, shouldering the door, with her heart beating fast.

Azor lay calm beside the stove.

You foolish girl! The fears are inside your head.

And Karlikov—it was so close. As soon as dawn had even thought of breaking, she would be away and safe.

Worse things could happen.

"Worse things can happen, Azor." She crouched down by him. "We must wait for dawn."

But the dog paid her no attention.

Out in the darkness something had stirred.

He pricked his ears. The hackles on his back like bristles.

He growled.

Low down in his chest.

Magda heard the pony stamping and snorting out under the trees.

She got up. Azor pushed his nose into the gap at the door, scrabbling at the earthen floor.

Heart thumping, Magda picked up a stick.

"What, Azor?"

She tried to listen. The dog squeezed out—leaping into the dark with teeth bared and hackles up. His long pale back disappeared under the trees.

"Azor!"

She stood trembling by the hut. A toothlike sliver of light fell out of the doorway and onto the snow.

She gripped the branch tight and crept out. Fear stabbed under her ribs. The pony whinnied and strained. The rope slipped from the tree.

"No!" Magda lunged for the trailing rein.

Hoofs thundered on the snow as the pony fled into the night.

Eyes crept close in the shadows of the forest.

Azor had heard. And smelled.

She heard scuffling. A yelp.

She swung about in the pitch-black. Peered into trees with terrified eyes. The dog barked, off under the trees. She thrashed the branch for all her life was worth. Flaying and thrashing, thrashing and flaying, beating the cold night, beating wildly at unseen teeth in every shadow.

The pony came crashing back through the undergrowth. Head flung high.

There was a yelping in the gloom. Snapping branches.

"Have mercy on me!" she wailed into the dark forest. "HAVE MERCY!"

5

"Hold that pony still!"

Magda gripped the branch and backed toward the hut. The pony snorted. The rope dangling loose from its halter.

"Who are you?" Magda yelled into the trees.

A boy stepped out of the darkness.

He was shapeless under the layers of a long heavy coat. She saw the glint of a gun in his hands and Azor at his heels.

"The w-wolf—" Magda stammered.

The boy looked at her. Glanced about under the trees. He rested his gun, grabbed the pony's rein.

And laughed.

His laugh was loud and long.

Magda did not understand.

"Are there more?" she said fearfully.

"Shh!" The boy held up his hand. Peered into the darkness. He raised the gun to his shoulder. Whispered under his breath. *"Pamirti vovk."* He took aim.

"Bang!" he shouted.

Magda jumped in her boots. The pony shied.

The boy laughed again.

Magda stared at him. "But the wolves—"

"Let me in, girl. I'm freezing out here."

He tied the pony to a nearby tree and pushed his way past her into the hut, threw a small bag down on the floor, and crouched by the fire.

The boy had a fur hat on his head, cheap Russian coypu, like the ones you could buy at Sanok market. His eyes were partly hidden in its shadows, but she could see they were sharp enough. Sheepskin mittens dangled on strings from the ends of his coat sleeves. The hands holding the gun were gaunt and strong. His leather boots were tatty and tied round with thick, blackened string.

He pulled off his hat—he was seventeen, maybe eighteen years old and a mass of straw-colored hair fell out like a halo in the firelight. He broke some sticks and threw them onto the fire, rubbed his hands in its heat.

"You have food?" he said.

"But—the wolves?"

"There are no wolves."

"No wolves?"

"You are a foolish girl."

"I am not a foolish girl. I thought it was a wolf. Kowalski said the wolves—"

But she did feel foolish all of a sudden.

"If you hadn't been so lucky to have me following you, you would have been screeching for mercy under the trees all night."

Magda closed the door angrily. "You have been following me?"

"I meant to take some food when you slept."

"How long have you been following me?"

"Since the village by the river," he said. "But I wasn't so stupid as to try and travel along the road."

Azor lay down beside him. The boy scratched at his obliging head. "You must have something?"

"Yes. I'm not so foolish as to leave home without something to eat."

"All right, all right. Just give me some. I'm starving."

Magda unwrapped the ham from its cloth and held it out to him. The boy laid the gun across his knees and tore at the meat with his teeth.

"I have a knife," she said.

He looked up. "Just get more wood on the fire."

"You're lucky I made a fire, aren't you?"

He waved his hand.

"You got any bread?"

"No."

He gestured at her rucksack. "What then?"

"Oats. I have oats and potatoes."

He pulled a small tin pan from his pack.

"Here. Make a kasha."

"Make your own!"

"You'll make it better."

He smiled and their eyes locked as he held the pan out. She pulled it away from him, knelt down, and filled it with oats.

The boy grinned to himself and wiped his greasy mouth with his sleeve. "I knew you'd have something good—"

She balanced the pan on top of the tiny stove and stirred the porridge angrily with a stick. The frown deepened on her face. The fear she had felt only moments before welled up inside her. Tears threatened; her hand stopped stirring.

The boy laughed. "You'll burn it if you don't pay attention."

Magda threw the stick down. "Why did you come if you only want to laugh at me?"

"Pah! You are a foolish girl." He stood up and stirred the porridge himself. "I was only on your path. And you have things to eat and saved me from making a fire. There. It's ready." He held it out. "Have some. Then you can sleep. I'll keep watch."

"Sleep! How do I know you won't steal the pony?"

"Well. I give you my word."

"Why should I believe you?"

"Because I am Ivan Rublev."

He said it as if it should mean something. As if his name was all that was needed.

"Well, I am Magda Krol," said Magda. "And I don't see why I should trust you."

There was something unfathomable in his eyes. And his face cracked and he laughed again. "God have mercy on me—Have mercy, have mercy! Ha ha!"

Magda grew as red as a cooked beetroot. The feeling spread right down to the tips of her toes.

"I was frightened." She spat out her embarrassment.

"You were screeching into the trees like a little girl." He slurped some porridge into his mouth with the stick. "Not bad—"

"I thought there was a wolf! May God have mercy on *you*, Ivan Rublev!"

It didn't come out the way she had intended. It sounded as if she meant some good. But she hadn't. He was objectionable. And arrogant. And rude. And she did not trust him.

"You're just tired," he said.

"I'm not afraid of you. Whoever you are. This is my hut. I found it, and I made the fire."

"Go on. Sleep. I won't hurt you." He smiled. "And eat something. Here."

She took the pan because she was hungry. And because her pride did not stretch that far.

The boy sat and stared at the fire, musing to himself.

They didn't speak, but she looked at the side of his face in the firelight sometimes.

Stupid, arrogant boy. With a cheap fur hat!

Magda lay on the bench and pulled the blanket over her shoulders.

Let him see I am not afraid. I will close my eyes, but I will not sleep. Let him try to steal my food. Let him see I am not a foolish girl!

• • •

But she *was* a foolish girl and she *did* fall asleep.

• • •

So she never heard Ivan Rublev tending the fire. Never heard him cutting branches outside or melting snow in his pan to drink. She never heard him emptying her pack in the low light of the fire, counting the goods inside. Halving them with an impressive degree of fairness. And she never heard him lay another blanket over her as she slept, laughing to himself, *havemercy, havemercy.*

6

Magda woke with the cold biting at her back. She got up and stumbled outside with the blanket around her shoulders.

The snow had stopped falling. It lay thick and new across the ground. Her laces trailed in it and she bent down to tie them.

"Ivan?" she called, her breath misting the still air.

Early light had begun to grow in the sky. Stars fading. A pale rim to the east. The cobweb of bare trees silhouetted against it.

"Ivan?"

But the boy had gone.

She pulled the blanket tight, shivering.

I am Ivan Rublev indeed! You were right not to trust him—

The pony rubbed its strong head against her side, smearing the blanket with hairs. He hadn't taken the pony at least.

"Not far now, the village is only on the other side of the forest. And Karlikov too." She scratched between the pony's ears. "Azor?" She peered into the trees. "Azor?"

What a worthless creature he was. She had fed him with her own hands. Fed him with her own food. And now he was gone.

A bird flitted to a tree close by. Dipped and chirruped.

What had the boy been doing out here?

Brunon Dudek had told her of the forest spirit Lesh-ee who lived among the roots of the Great Tree of the World.

When she was younger, before Babula had told her about his ways, she had liked to go to Brunon Dudek's woodshed and frighten herself hearing his old stories as he plucked chickens and gulped at a bottle of vodka.

"When the wind whistles through them trees and you find yourself lost in the woods and you can't find your way home, Lesh-ee will appear, with his horns and his shaggy coat. Watch out! He'll lead you further and further from home—to the swamps and the *dark places*! You mustn't follow him, but take off your clothes, and turn them inside out, and put your left shoe on your right foot, and your right shoe on your left foot, and use your own head. Don't listen to what he tells you. Gggrh!"

"Enough, Brunon Dudek!"—Babula's shadow falling in the doorway. "Stop listening to that godless drunken fool, Magda."

"Ach, Agnieszka, there's nothing wrong with the old stories—"

• • •

Magda looked out from under the trees.

There were footprints in the snow leading away from the hut. They did not take the wide-open path but disappeared between the tree trunks. Where was the boy going? Magda wondered. He had not asked her where *she* was going. He had been as unsurprised to find her as if she had been a fallen branch on the ground.

She went back into the hut and rolled up the blankets. She discovered her pilfered bag.

The worthless. Arrogant. Thief. You blushed! And made him porridge!

She stamped about the hut, thrusting things angrily into the bag. She kicked at the door that would not open without force. And hurt her toe.

If I ever find him I'll—She felt her faith flutter for a moment. *Two days ago your own village was filled with people, and now it seems that everyone has forgotten you. Even that wretched dog.*

For some reason that she could not understand, Magda wished the boy had not left her. She looked up into the branches above her, arching into the brightening sky like beams. She remembered Ivan's long laugh.

Why do you care? He is a worthless creature—no better than the dog. She untied the pony and climbed onto its back, kicking it on with unease lodged in her heart. She headed along the foresters' track running straight and wide through the trees. The sooner she reached the open fields above Karlikov the better. To see a house, even empty, would be something.

Her hands gripped the wiry mane. The pony's head rose and fell as it tramped through the snow, ears flicking back as she chivvied it on. Northwards. With thoughts of Ivan Rublev mocking her in the dark.

Have mercy. Have mercy.

• • •

By mid-morning Magda had reached the fringes of the forest, and below her the roofs of Karlikov were shining in a weak sunlight that glanced over the hilltops.

A fresh-smelling wind whipped lazy trails of snow across the surface of the fields. She clapped her hands together in the cold. "You see, it wasn't far." She rubbed the pony's neck. In the distance—a dark speck against the white—was a truck, moving slowly along a road.

"Hey!" She kicked the pony on, with the reins flapping and her arms waving and everything grim forgotten. "Hey!" she shouted out across the fields. "Hey. Wait for me!"

Her heart beat fast as she picked along the ditches and drifted hedgerows and lost sight of the rooftops. Urgency pounded inside her like a drum. She called again, as loud as she could: "Wait for me. Wait for me!"

The pony slid onto the hard-packed snow of a road. She forced it onward with her coat flapping and her legs aching.

Rounding a shallow bend, two figures came into view. She called out. "Hello. Wait for me."

The figures turned: an old man and his wife leading a donkey. And there was Azor, snuffling along the side of the drifts.

"Azor!"

He wagged his faithless tail. Magda jumped down from the pony.

"Who on heaven's earth are you, girl?" the old woman said.

"Magda Krol. From Morochov."

"Morochov? You missed the trucks or what?" said the old man.

"I came across the hill, yesterday. On the pony."

The dog stuck its nose into Magda's leg.

"Shoo!" The old woman flapped her arm. "That dog's been following us like the devil!"

45

"No, it is all right. He ran off this morning. It's Bogdan Stopko's dog."

"Pan Stopko?" said the old man. "Where have they taken him?"

"I don't know. I was hiding in my grandmother's cellar. I saw nothing. Just heard on the radio—"

"Where is your grandmother now?" said the old woman.

"Dead."

"In the snow?"

"No. The priest came. It was before they took everyone away."

"Thanks be to God in heaven," said the old woman, crossing herself.

"But where are the trucks? I saw one from up there on the hill." Magda pointed up to the distant line of trees high above the village. "Where are they taking us? Am I too late?"

"No. We must go to the village," said the man. "You aren't too late, girl." He put his hands up, looked skyward. "Where they're taking us—that's another question." He picked up his bag and slung it over his shoulder.

"But what's the reason?" said Magda, falling in step.

"They say it's the weather," muttered the old woman, plodding on, with the donkey dragging behind her. "We don't understand it, but we're too old to hold up our arms and ask questions. The soldiers came and told us to leave. We must pray that everything will return to normal soon."

Up ahead more villagers appeared, tramping along the track with crates of chickens and canvas bags and badly tied belongings. Several decrepit wooden cottages came into view, ramshackle behind rickety fences. And with relief Magda saw an army van further along, exhaust fumes smoking on the cold air.

A group of villagers had stopped to watch an old man arguing with two soldiers.

"I am not leaving. Get off my porch!"

The old man raised his voice, pushed at one of the soldiers.

They dragged him down the steps. "You have to come. We have orders!"

"Get your hands off me. This is my property. Get your hands off."

The assembled villagers looked on like cattle in the field. But their voices grew angry, the old women muttering, "For shame, for shame."

Behind them another van slid and grumbled along the track before coming to a halt. A young soldier jumped from the cab with a gun slung across his back. Open-handed he beckoned. "Come. This way. You must get in the trucks. All of you."

The villagers did not move. Old men began remonstrating. "What about the animals? I won't leave my donkey."

"Where are we going?"

"We have our orders," the soldier said. "Now don't cause us trouble. You'll be safer with us. You will be compensated for the animals."

"What about my donkey?"

"Orders are orders, Grandfather. Everyone is to be evacuated."

A freezing wind blew down from the hill, ruffling the fur on the soldier's hat. He was unshaven. He looked tired. Like he had cajoled too many from their villages already. From villages they had never left in their lives.

The old women were pushed up into the back of the truck, large skirted behinds clambering up the steps. The old men would accept no helping hands. They argued over the seizing of their animals. A soldier kicked at Azor. The dog skittered away, whimpering. Crates of chickens were handed up to eager old hands, bags grabbed over the tailgate.

At the back of the truck another soldier took Magda's pony, noted something down on a clipboard. Blowing on his fingers he asked her name, her village. He stamped the paper, ripped a sheet, and handed it to her.

"You'll get compensation."

There was shouting and complaining.

"What about my donkey? What are you going to do with it? You can't take my livestock from me!"

"You'll get compensation, Grandfather. In you get."

Magda rubbed the pony's nose. It bowed its head a little, pushed against her.

"Come on, girl. Up you get."

She clambered into the truck. "What are you going to do with him? He's a good pony."

"You'll get compensation like the others. Just take that paper to the authorities in Krakow."

"Krakow!"

There was a sudden outcry among the villagers.

"Krakow? What will I do there? I have no family there."

The murmuring became desperate and fearful. Old women began crying. "Let us off to die in peace!"

Azor sat in the snow, watching from a distance. Magda wished he had gone with the boy now.

The soldiers began to close the doors.

"Come on. Sit down. Get yourselves comfortable. It will be all right."

Clang.

There was a sudden silence in the darkness. Magda could hear the breathing of twenty souls.

She pushed her face to a crack in the doors. Peered with one eye, her hands spread on the boards.

A soldier talking on the roadside. He led Stopko's pony to the edge of the track. She squinted. He pulled something from his belt. Raised his hand to the side of the pony's head.

Crack!

The pony fell on its knees. A bloody red hole in its head. Its breath labored. Mouth open. Blood on its tongue. Then over it fell.

She pulled her head back.

"What? What did you see, girl?"

It was the old man.

"They are shooting the ponies. Shooting the ponies." She felt her body tremble. Her legs weakened. The engine grew louder and with a lurch Magda fell against the wall.

"Sit down, girl. Sit down." Old hands helped her along. She picked her way over the legs and bags. The villagers becoming silent like sheep to slaughter.

She found a place at the back of the truck and sat down. She put her trembling hands in her lap. Pulled off her gloves so she could feel her own flesh. Above her a small panel in the roof let in weak gray light. Against her shoulder a body moved, and she looked at the person leaning in the corner beside her.

Her heart jumped a beat.

Ivan Rublev!

7

The smell of onions and unwashed winter clothes rose from the frightened old villagers on the floor of the truck. Even the chickens were quiet. It was not what Magda had imagined.

That picture of Stopko's pony sinking in the snow with a round bloody hole between its eyes—

She looked at Ivan Rublev's face, undisturbed in the dingy light. There was a smudge of blood at the corner of his mouth. She shook him by the shoulder. "Ivan." She managed to pull him up straight. "Ivan."

His eyes opened.

"It's me. The girl from the forest."

He looked at her. Rubbed his head. "Where am I?" He looked about at the old villagers. Then at her again. "It's you, Havemercy. Where are we?"

"They're taking us to Krakow."

"I have to get out."

"Sit down. You can't get out. What happened to you?"

He rubbed his head a little. "Those pigs took my gun. The best gun. How long have we been going?"

"I'm not sure."

He waved his hand about. "Who are these people?"

"Villagers," she whispered. "The villagers from Karlikov."

"And your pony?"

"They shot him. They say I will get compensation. But it was Stopko's pony, not mine."

"Stopko?"

"A man from my village."

"I'm surprised at you, Havemercy."

"Stop calling me that."

"All right, all right. I just didn't think you looked like a horse thief."

"I'm not. I was trying to get to Karlikov."

"Well, you did that well enough. Now look what's happened. You should have stayed at home."

"But I have to find the others. So I can go back."

"Listen—" He turned to her. Some of the old people were looking at him as they bumped along. He lowered his voice. "You won't be going back—"

"What do you mean?"

"It's not just here. It's everywhere. What do you think it's like in the cities? They've got no wood to burn. No chickens. No cellars."

"I don't understand."

"They say it's going to get worse. That it's not going to end. And now all the borders are closing. I've seen it. Soon they won't have fuel for all these trucks and for keeping people warm. There are soldiers stationed on all the roads east. There is going to be war. That's why they're taking everyone while they can."

"But why us? We villagers can get by. We always do."

"For how long, Havemercy? How long before people come from the cities to steal your chickens? The soldiers will be the first. And then it will be village against village."

"The village people don't behave like that. The winters always come. And then they go. Soon it will be spring."

But she remembered the raids on Zborov last winter, the old men getting their guns ready.

"God will watch over us," she murmured, looking at her hands.

"God?" Ivan snorted in derision.

Magda remembered that last call to her mother. *Even the English are hungry. It is getting ugly, Magda . . . I cannot find a way back.*

She looked at him. "How can you know all this? Why should I believe you?"

"You're just a foolish country girl who leads her pony through the drifts and gets stuck in the back of this truck and thinks God is watching over her."

"Well, if you are so clever, how did you find yourself in this truck too?"

"I was trying to steal food from the soldiers. Camped a bit west from here. They caught me." He banged his fist angrily against the side of the truck.

"Shh!" said Magda. Some of the villagers were looking again. She took a jar from her bag. "Here, have something to eat."

Ivan pulled off his gloves, cracked the lid, and took some pickled mushrooms out with his fingers.

"And why did you take my dog?" Magda said.

"I didn't. He followed me." Ivan's mouth was full. "I couldn't stop him." He put up his hands in defense. "Honest!"

"I don't know if anything you say is true."

"Suit yourself."

He settled himself in the corner.

• • •

Krakow—Magda had been there once, with her mother. She remembered the cars and the people and the noise. She remembered Mama buying her an ice cream. It fell from her hands and she cried and Mama bent down and said, "Don't worry, Magda," and she bought her another from the ice-cream man, who stuck a chocolate stick into it and told her not to cry over spilled milk and laughed. She remembered that.

She thought of her mother. Far away in England. She thought of what the boy had said. They were closing the borders; they would not be allowed back to the village.

How could all this happen because of winter?

• • •

Eventually there came the sound of other engines and horns blowing and the spray of slush against the wheels. They had reached the outskirts of Krakow at last.

Bolts scraped back and the tailgate opened. Daylight flooded into the truck. The villagers burst into railing and complaining—the women grabbing at the arms of their men.

"Ivan—" Magda reached out for him. "Ivan."

He looked down at her hand on his arm.

"I am afraid," she said.

"That won't help you, Havemercy."

Magda took her hand away.

"Come on," he said, pulling her up. "It won't be that bad. Just keep your eyes open. And follow me. And don't let go of your food. Or that paper for the pony."

"Out you get," said a soldier.

"You are treating us like cattle!" shouted an old man. "Where are we going to stay?"

"They took my donkey," said another. "How am I going to get compensation?"

"Don't worry, Grandpa. You will be looked after."

The weary villagers found themselves inside a snow-blown courtyard enclosed by wire fences. The courtyard was surrounded on two sides by low buildings, and the banks of metal-framed windows reflected only a grimness of gray and ice. Bored-looking soldiers manned the entrance gates.

"Patience, patience. We have beds for you. If you have relatives, you will be able to go to them. Now, come down slow and orderly. We are here to help. Hand me your bags. No need to worry, no need to worry, Babcia," said the soldier.

Magda and Ivan jumped down onto the snow.

"Who are you with, children?"

"Nobody," Magda said.

"That boy wasn't with her," said the driver of the truck, pointing at Ivan. "We caught him in our camp. Trying to steal food." He grabbed Ivan's arm. "He had a gun."

"Where are you from, boy?" The soldier's face turned hard.

Magda stepped up. "He's—he's my brother. We were separated after they took the villagers. It was my father's gun. He is Ivan Krol. I am Magda Krol. From Morochov."

Another truck came grumbling into the courtyard. It ground its way through the icy ruts, sounding its horn loudly.

The driver climbed up on the step to the cab.

"Well, just keep your eye on him, soldier—"

Out on the snow a man was sitting behind a small table. The villagers crowded around him impatiently. Magda and Ivan were marched to the front.

"Two unescorted children."

The official looked up from his work, stamped his cold feet under the table.

"Names?" His lips were dry and cracked.

"Magda and Ivan Krol. From Morochov," said Magda.

"Parents?"

"Just my mother, Maria Krol."

"Is she on another convoy?"

"She is in England," said Magda. "I need to call her."

The man looked up again. "Any other relatives?"

"No. I must find Bogdan Stopko from Morochov."

She was aware of her shabby winter coat all of a sudden. Of smelling of smoke and winter clothes, her hands dirty, her hair unwashed.

The man wrote something down. "You'll have to go to Bartholomew."

"Bartholomew?"

"Displaced children's center here in Nova Huta. Over there." He pointed to the door of a building. "Wait in there for the transport." He waved them away gruffly.

• • •

Ivan scanned the courtyard. Looked at the high gates closing behind the trucks.

"We have to get out of here."

"How?" Magda said.

"Leave it to me."

"But they'll help us, won't they?"

"You don't understand anything."

She followed him across the yard to the doors of the building. Inside, it was painted like the school in Karlikov. Official paint— gray-green to shoulder height and white above. There were grubby streaks of hand marks against the wall. They sat on a wooden bench. Alone in a bare, echoing room.

"When we get our chance," Ivan said, under his breath, "we'll run."

"Why? How will we find somewhere to stay if we run?" Magda said. "At least it is warm here."

"I can look after myself."

Magda shifted on her seat. Stared out the grimy window.

Somewhere in the building a door slammed.

"Where have you come from, Ivan?"

"The Ukrainian border."

"The Ukraine? That's so far away."

"Yes. And if you think it's bad here . . . just wait."

"My mother is in London," Magda said. "I need to find her."

"And you think they'll help you?"

"Why wouldn't they?"

"Trust me." Ivan looked out the window, his gray eyes distant. He closed them. "You have no friends here."

Then he crossed his feet at the ankle and folded his arms over his chest, crushing his hat underneath them. Opening one eye, he said: "I won't wait for you. When the chance comes."

• • •

Hours passed. In the fading light Magda waited fearfully, her hands nervous in her lap. She could not close her eyes like Ivan.

Finally a door at the back of the room opened: a large man leaned on the door handle and hung into the room. "This way." His voice echoed against the bare walls.

Ivan sat up, unfolded his crumpled hat, put it on, and picked up his bag. The man ushered them silently through dimly lit corridors. Unlocked a set of doors. Icy steps led up onto the dark street.

The cold night air hit them in the face. A small minibus was idling by the side of the road. A man was leaning against it, smoking.

"Two more for Bartholomew, Jan," the guard called across the street.

Magda's heart beat fast. The man by the minibus beckoned.

Ivan said to follow. If he runs, should you go too? But then you will never hear of Stopko and the others.

"Now, Magda!"

And Ivan ducked and jumped a heap of snow and ran. She had

no time to think. The guard grabbed her shoulder. There was only the driver—smoking by the van. He was not expecting it.

"Hey!" He dropped his cigarette and gave chase.

But he was too slow.

Ivan ran between the buildings, leaping nimbly over the banks of snow with his heavy coat flapping and his hat pulled low. Running leaping stumbling: for one second he turned his head. "*Magda!*" he shouted.

"Ivan!"

But Ivan had disappeared into the shadows beneath a block of flats, and was gone.

The driver shouted and swore in the darkness.

"Stupid bugger!" He bent over coughing. "He won't get far." He pulled a mobile phone out of his pocket. "Hello. Hello. Jan over at thirty-four. Displaced youth's just done a runner. Don't know. No. About seventeen." He looked at Magda. "Yeah. All right, I won't be long." He put the phone back into his pocket. "Don't you go getting any clever ideas. It'll be minus twenty tonight. In you get."

He slid open the door of the minibus and helped her up into the back. There were other children sitting inside. The windows were thick with frozen condensation.

Magda found a place. Squeezed onto the cold vinyl bench between the bundled coats of the others. She peered out the windows as the door slid shut. She wondered about the dog, Azor. Was he still waiting on the side of the road? Waiting for everyone to come home. And Ivan? But if he had made it from the Ukraine in this weather he would be all right.

The engine started with a judder. She felt a numb weariness. It wasn't just the cold.

She sat silent as the bus made its way through the warren of buildings on the Nova Huta estate, with banks of dark windows in every block of flats like blind sentinels. They passed vehicles creeping along the icy streets, fat snowflakes flashing in glaring headlights. It felt a very long way from home.

Eventually they pulled up in front of a two-story building. The driver jumped down from the cab and slid open the door. It scraped and clunked into place. "We're here. Come on, there'll be something to eat." He helped them down.

A woman from the building stood out on the snow and beckoned to the line of disoriented children. They filed in through the door and found themselves in a chilly entrance lobby with a high desk that ran along one wall. The desk was covered in files and paperwork, and on the wall a faded poster proclaimed:

Their Future, Foster a Child Today.

The woman led them across the hallway and opened a door into a large room with benches lined up across the floor.

"Quiet now—it won't take long. Then you can have a bit to eat and get to bed. I need to take your names."

A small boy started crying.

Magda felt it too. She reached out for the boy and he slid up onto her lap. With every nerve in her body she wanted to be back in the village: to smell Babula's kitchen, hear the tick of the clock on the shelf, crawl under the heavy blankets on her bed, fall asleep listening to the logs collapsing in the stove.

The woman wrote down their names and villages in a large book.

"Now, let's get something for you to eat and I'll take you upstairs. Your parents will probably arrive tomorrow."

The lights went out.

There were loud exclamations that sounded from other parts of the building, shrieks and laughter. The woman fumbled her way out of the room. They heard her talking to someone in the entrance hall. "It's getting earlier every day. Do you know where the paraffin is?"

A door closed. The children were left alone, hiding their snuffling fears in the dark. Then there were footsteps and the striking of a match and the woman reappeared with a small lamp glowing in her hand.

"Are the lights going to come back on?" one of the girls asked.

"Not tonight. But you'll get used to it. Now let's get some food. This way. You older ones, help the little ones. Watch out for the steps."

• • •

In a dimly lit room, sitting in rows on long hard benches, they ate some sausage and bread. The sausage was fatty and hard. There was milk for the smaller children and tea for everyone else.

Magda could hear the sound of footsteps on the floor above. When they had eaten, they made their way up the stairs, following the woman and her lamp along a corridor.

"These are the sinks." She waved her hand at an open door. Children were standing at a row of sinks, little ones on tiptoes, big ones looking at the new arrivals.

"The hot water only comes on for a few hours in the morning, so no wasting time. Here we are."

She pushed open a door to a long room with metal bunkbeds jammed so close you could barely walk between them. Paraffin lamps hung from the ceiling. The air smelled bitter with smoke. There were children everywhere, climbing into bunks, sitting on the beds, talking in the aisles.

"Quiet down! Now come on, girls—find a spare bed. You older ones can help the little ones get ready. Make sure they keep their belongings under the pillow."

And with those words she turned and left.

• • •

The children climbed into their beds. Magda had not undressed, but lay on the narrow metal bunk, her thoughts drifting.

Far off, away across some remembered meadow, across a wide sea of rippling grass, a bell was ringing. But Magda could not tell from which direction the sound came, or which path led home. Home to good sensible Babula, with a cool, soft hand on her brow: *The wind blows where it chooses, but we never know where it comes from, or where it is going. We are just one more stalk amongst that swaying grass. One more stalk. Not the first. Not the last.*

Magda thought of the boy, Ivan, running into the dark. Magda did not know why Ivan was running. Or what had happened to him.

It bothered her.

And Mama. How far away London seemed.

And even if the authorities found Bogdan Stopko, would he come looking for her? She turned on her side with her hand under her head.

She was a pulled tooth. Rootless. Alone.

A landed fish thrashing on the bank.

8

It happened then, that three weeks later—without warning— Bogdan Stopko arrived at Bartholomew Displaced Children's Center.

Thinner and paler, Magda stood awkwardly in the cold hallway. "Pan Stopko!"

Stopko did not look like the man she had known in Morochov. He bowed his head. Muttered. Averted his eyes. Hid his dirty hands in the hat he held in front of him. The director of the children's home led them to a room and left them alone.

"How did you find me?" Magda said.

"A boy I did not know told me that you were looking for me." Stopko sat down on a chair. Looked about the bare room to avoid her eyes. "He told me where to find you."

"Ivan!"

"He didn't tell me his name. I didn't ask."

"It must be. But where are the others from the village?"

"Kowalski had family in Lodz. He went there with his wife somehow. The others, I—I don't know now."

"The Dudek brothers?"

"Aleksy has work at the Zory coal mine. Same as me."

"Brunon?" she asked.

"Brunon? I don't know where he is. Why didn't you come with us that night? Did you bury your grandmother, girl?"

"I was frightened when I saw the men. And I hid in the cellar. Yes, I buried Babula."

"Have you called your mother?"

"I have tried every day. They only let me make one call—but her telephone is always dead. They don't help me. They know I am sixteen. They say they cannot let me stay here forever. The other children. Their parents come. They have been split up on the transports or they have family. But for me there's no one."

Magda's voice broke and she hung her head. She couldn't help herself.

Stopko, fiddling with his hat, looked embarrassed. "Come on now. Crying won't help."

Magda looked up, wiped her eyes. "I have a paper for your pony."

"My pony?"

"Yes. I took the pony from your barn. And your dog. To get to Karlikov. That's where I found the trucks."

"A paper?"

"Yes. You will get compensation."

"Why?"

"They shot it." She wiped her nose on her sleeve, took the folded paper from her pocket. Handed it to him.

"How much?" he said.

"I don't know. They told me to take the paper. That's all."

Stopko folded it up and put it inside his jacket. Pulled on his hat and got up from his chair.

Magda reached out for his arm. "Please. You will help me?"

"Look, Magda, I am sleeping in a room with five other men. What can I do for you?"

"Please, Pan Stopko. I have no one else. You cannot leave me here."

"But I don't have anywhere for you to stay. You can't share a room with five men."

"Then help me get to England?"

"Listen to me, girl." He pointed his stubby finger at her. "In Morochov I knew everything. Here I am just another hungry man from the countryside. I don't understand it any better than you. But something has changed. They talk about war. We're not the only ones without electricity or food. They say troops are moving east. They have taken eastern Kazakhstan. Some say the Russians won't stop until they cross the border into Poland."

"But why?"

"The only thing I know is that there are soldiers on every road from here to the Ukraine. You won't get back to the village, much less to London."

"What will I do then?"

He turned and stared out the window. "I will give you half the money for the pony. I owe it to you."

"Is that all?"

Stopko put up his hands. "I can't do anything else, Magda. I'm lucky enough to have a bed. And work that buys me a bit of food. If I could go back home, I would go back yesterday."

"You are just going to leave me here?"

Bogdan Stopko was regretting his promise to give Magda half the money. She was, well—not quite nothing to him. But times had changed. Nevertheless, some part of his conscience stirred.

"Listen. The other men have gone to the coal mines at Zory for their week's shift. Tonight there is a bed and I will let you sleep and eat for one night. You can queue for the money. But after that I'll be gone to Zory too. You'll have to look after yourself."

• • •

Before they left, Bogdan Stopko had to sign a paper saying he had taken her. He did not want to do it. He had to write his address. His cheeks became red. The woman opened the book for him. Showed him where to write. His writing was like a child's.

• • •

"It's a long walk. Can't afford a bus for two," he said when they were out on the street.

Magda pulled her hat down. Slung her small bag over her shoulder. "I don't mind a walk," she said quickly.

"Hmm. Well, don't bother me if you get tired."

A small minibus loaded with people sloshed past them, spraying dirty snow from its wheels. The people inside were packed like mushrooms in a jar, bodies squashed against the steamy windows with bulging bags heavy on their laps.

"Come on. This way."

Stopko stepped out onto the road and strode across it with his square-fingered hands in his pockets and his big square neck deep in his collar. And she slogged along behind him.

9

Bogdan Stopko was right. In Morochov he had been someone, and here he was just another man from the countryside. The city people, if they looked at all, looked distrustfully at the stocky man, and the thin country girl trotting at his heels.

At last, they crossed the river. Tramped the cobbled pavements with houses leaning over them on every side. Stopko halted at a shabby building with a wooden door. He opened it with a key on a string in his pocket. From a dingy stone-flagged hallway he scuffed wearily up the creaking stairs, his short, dirty fingers clenching the dark banister. At the top of the landing he opened a door.

"This is it."

Magda stepped inside a stale-smelling room, and Stopko let the door fall shut behind them.

Ill-sorted beds were pushed against the walls. A large iron radiator under the window was covered in damp woolen socks. In the corner was a bathroom sink, an unframed mirror above it, a brown stain on the enamel under the taps. A melamine cupboard, attempting mahogany, clung lopsided to the wall. Underneath it on a small table was a battered kettle with a grimy handle, an empty vodka bottle, and several dirty mugs. From under the covers on one of the beds a large shape was snoring loudly. Stopko waved at it. "Don't worry. Tomasz wouldn't wake up if you lit a fire on his head."

Magda looked around the room.

Well. It could be worse.

She remembered what the priest had said about Stopko, *Good men don't grow like brambles, Magda. He has two fields a tractor and a pony—*

She looked at Bogdan Stopko. He sat on the bed, wearily pulling off his wet boots—leaning them against the radiator. Brambles indeed. He saw her looking at him.

"You don't like it, huh?"

"No, no. It's not that. Just—"

"Just what?"

"Nothing. Nothing, Pan Stopko. Shall I make you a tea?"

"Yes. If there's electricity." He reached over and put his hand on the radiator. "There's heat so maybe there's power."

Magda put her bag down in the corner and took off her coat. Stopko waved at the door. She hung it on an overcrowded peg there. Went to the sink, filled up the kettle. "The tea, Pan Stopko?"

"In the saucer."

Magda looked down at the dirty table. There was an old saucer with a couple of used tea bags squashed onto it. The kettle started popping and crackling.

"Make one for yourself," Stopko said. "There's bread and sausage in the cupboard too."

They sat at each end of the bed and ate their meal. "I need to sleep," said Stopko, slurping at the tea. "I have to work tomorrow."

"But the paper. The money for the pony?"

"Yes. Yes." He dug the paper from his pocket. Held it out to her. "Half and half. Like we agreed."

She pulled it from his fingers. "But where do I take it?"

"The administrative building on the corner of Spinka Street. It's not far. Just ask." He leaned toward her, grasped her shoulder. Narrowed his eyes like a horse trader. "You come back with the money!"

"Of course, Pan Stopko."

"Mmm." He released his grip. "Take some food too. You'll be there all day."

"Pan Stopko. Do you—do you know where I can find Ivan?"

"Who?"

"The boy who told you where I was. Do you know where he is?"

"No."

"How did he find you?"

"I don't know, Magda. Now let me rest. I could sleep for a week and still be tired."

And with that he lay down, pulled the blankets over his head, and turned to the wall.

• • •

At the administrative building, Magda took a number from a roll of tickets and stood with the jostling crowd. She peered down at the ticket. Two hundred and ninety-three.

God in heaven.

At the far end of the room was a counter with one woman behind a window. One by one she shouted the numbers out.

People squabbled. There was a din in the cold, airless room, a din and the smell of unwashed bodies. A mobile phone rang. Someone shouted into it above the noise. A mother with two children tried to push to the front. An old woman with deep lines in her yellowing skin screeched angrily. The children cried.

. . .

At the end of a long day, Magda received three thousand zloty for Bogdan Stopko's dead pony. She folded the worn notes and stuffed them into her jacket. Pushed her way through the crowds.

Outside, it was dark already. She rested against a wall. Her feet, still damp from her long walk across the city, were frozen and aching.

There weren't many people about now. There were no lights. Shutters were closed.

A Jeep crawled along the icy street, its windows darkened. A fat woman, bottle in hand, stumbled about in the middle of the road, slipped onto her knees, gulped from the bottle.

Magda slunk quickly through the shadows. It wasn't far to Stopko's building. Her heart beat fast.

"Psst."

She jumped.

"Magda."

She peered into a gloomy doorway.

"Magda. It's me. Ivan."

"Ivan!"

"You have the money?"

"What?"

Ivan stepped out of the shadows. "The money for the pony?"

"Yes. But—how do you know? I mean, how did you know I would be here?"

"I've been following you. I followed that oaf Stopko to Nova Huta too. I'm freezing. You've been in there for hours. How much did they give you for the pony?"

"Three thousand."

"It's not much. But maybe it will be enough."

"Enough for what?"

"To get out of here, you foolish girl."

"You came to take my money?"

A smile cracked across Ivan's face in the shadowy doorway. He reached out and pulled Magda toward him. His hands were strong.

Maybe he is going to steal the money—

But Ivan Rublev leaned close and tried to kiss her.

"Get off!" Magda pushed him away.

He held her at arm's length, laughing.

Magda kicked at him.

"Hey, little horse thief. Have mercy!"

Magda snorted. Her face flushed. Still tight in his grip.

"Don't call me that again! Let me go!"

"Listen. I've found a way for us to get to England. Maybe."

"England?" Magda stopped kicking at him and he let her go.

"Yes. That's where you want to go, isn't it? Find your mother?"

"How?"

"There are people. We pay them. They find a way."

"But half of the money is Bogdan Stopko's."

"You're going to give half of the money to that square-headed oaf?"

"It was his pony. I promised him."

"His pony! He left it to starve. If you hadn't taken it, he would never have thought about it again."

"But I promised him."

Ivan grabbed her shoulder. "Listen." She tried to pull away. "Do you really think Stopko will even give you half? Hmm?"

"I—I—"

"The first night he will buy a woman—"

"How can you say such things?"

"—The first night he will buy a woman and a bottle of vodka—and in the morning they will all be gone. The woman, the vodka, and the money."

"But isn't it better to do what's right?"

"Fine. Take your money. Give it to Stopko. And then you can start praying. You'll need your prayers then!"

Magda looked at her feet. She thought of Babula safe in her grave. Of her mother.

"But why do *you* want to go to England, Ivan? What is there for you?"

"A job. I will get paid. Either you come with me or you don't. Your choice."

"And the money?" She clasped at her pocket.

"You still think I'll steal it? I told you before. I gave you my word in the forest."

"But you took half my food."

"Only half, Magda. Remember that."

The bundled zloty were burning a hole against her breast. Was this the right thing?

A police van trundled into sight at the end of the street. Ivan pulled her back into the shadows, his arm warm around her chest.

She thought about Stopko, happy to leave her in Nova Huta. Of his pony, left in the barn. Of its blood on the snow. And the dog. Stopko hadn't even asked about his dog.

The crow was not really a crow, Magda—Babula tapping a finger on the side of her nose—*but only the girl could see a light behind those beady eyes.*

"Yes, Ivan," Magda said, turning her head against him and looking up. "I will go to England with you."

10

There was a small pile of handguns on a low table. Three dark-haired men slouched on a sofa. One of them played with his mobile phone. The other two sat bored, fiddling with the large gold rings on their fingers, shoeless feet stretched out on the patterned carpet. In the corner a music video played silently on a television. Girls gyrated on the screen. The room was thick with cigarette smoke. Coming up through the floor was the *boom boom* of music from a club downstairs.

Comfortably filling a heavy armchair was a fat man with dark stubble on his cheeks, a large belly stretching the seams of his immaculate suit.

The man stood up, smiling, opened his arms. *"Parev, Ivan! Kak ti?"* He had a big voice, and his confident smile flashed a row of gold fillings.

Sitting on the arm of the chair, a thin blond girl picked at her fingernails. The fat man waved at her. "Tanya—" She got up with a blank face and left the room. "Ivan. So. What have you got for me tonight?"

"Greetings, Valentin—" Ivan clasped his hand. They embraced.

Magda stood quietly like Ivan had said she should.

. . .

"Don't speak, Magda. Let me do the talking."

"Where are we going?"

"Some friends. They can help us."

"Who are they?"

"Armenians, from the Ukraine."

"Armenians?"

"I can't go to the Albanians with a girl. Just let me do the talking—and hide five hundred in your belt."

. . .

The fat bandit looked at Magda. Magda shifted uneasily.

"It's about the job," said Ivan. "I want to take it."

"Ha!" The fat man laughed. "How much money have you got?"

"Two thousand."

"Two thousand! That won't cover it. How do I know you will deliver?"

"Come on, Valentin. I need your help. We can take a truck, a container. Anything."

"Mmm. Two thousand is nothing, Ivan. You have papers?"

"No."

"But without papers . . . How do I know you won't get caught when you get there?"

"I won't get caught. You know me."

"Maybe. But the girl. It's not enough money. You know it."

"Maybe I can find another five hundred," Ivan said.

"Why not stay here, Ivan? There's money to be made. There are a million girls." He rubbed his stomach. "I can use you here."

"But I need the money now."

"Money," said the fat man, grinning again. "If I was you, I'd head east. That's where the money's going. But why the girl?"

"She helped me. It's a debt—of honor."

The man sat down heavily, twisted the gold watch on his wrist. "Mmm." He leaned forward with his hands on his knees. "But I want three thousand—call it my insurance against your return. It's an important job. And I won't be happy if you don't deliver." His eyes were hard black pinpricks in the dim light of the room.

"Two and a half, Valentin."

They stared at each other.

The fat man slapped his hands on his thighs and laughed. "You are a wolf, Ivan. A real Ukrainian wolf!"

"It's a deal then?"

"I will see what I can do."

"We want to go soon."

The man stabbed his pudgy gold-encrusted hand into his chest. "I say when."

"But soon?"

"Maybe." He coughed heavily. "Now, the money."

"Now?"

"Yes, now." He clicked his fingers. "Nazar."

One of the men on the sofa looked up, stopped playing with his phone.

Ivan pulled out the zloty from his coat. The man slowly counted the notes, passed them to Valentin.

"Two and a half, boss."

"Okay. Listen to me, little wolf," said Valentin. "I have a truck going to a place in London, to someone I know. From there you will have to find your way to Liverpool. It is a town in the north. Go to the Armenian church, the Holy Trinity, and ask the priest there for Tony Gulbekhian. Gulbekhian will take the package from you. You will get your money back when you return to Krakow. Plus another four thousand for your work. In yuan."

"Only four thousand?"

"In *yuan*, Ivan. That is the deal."

"And how will I get back?"

"Gulbekhian will arrange it. If you do this job well, I will find other things for you. More money, little wolf." The fat man's mobile started buzzing on the table. "I'll send Nazar. Don't let me down, Ivanchik. With a pretty girl like that to distract you." He waved his hand toward the door and answered his phone. *"Da!"*

• • •

"How did you know he would accept two and a half?" Magda said when they were clear of the flashing doorway and back down the street.

"I know these people, Magda. I know how their minds work. If there wasn't something in it for Valentin, he wouldn't have helped."

"What package have you got to take?"

"Fake passports."

"Why passports?"

"People want to get east. They are valuable documents."

"Why does he trust you?"

"Why do you, Magda?"

. . .

She followed him through the darkened streets of Krakow, the hard wedge of remaining zloty rubbing against her breast. She did not know where she was going and—she did not know why she trusted him.

Bogdan Stopko will be waiting. He will be sitting on his bed with a dark crease on his forehead thinking that he has been robbed. Robbed by Agnieszka Krol's granddaughter.

Even though Ivan had spoken words that seemed to live with a certain truth, about Stopko and his money and how the pony would have died forgotten in the village anyway, even so—

In her mind there was only one truth. And she had given her word to Bogdan Stopko. Ivan had twisted her thoughts.

"How will we know when we can leave?" Magda asked.

"They'll tell us. Don't worry."

"You already gave them Stopko's money. How do you know they won't cheat us?"

"Stop punching yourself about that oaf Stopko. He wouldn't expect any less."

"But he would! You don't know how people live in our village. He would not expect me to cheat him."

"Listen, Magda. You have eyes in your head. Look about. Doesn't everything look different to you? Hasn't it all changed?"

Fear had stripped Magda's certainty away. She felt it melting from her bones. She did not know what would be left when it had gone. What bit of her would remain standing.

"Come on." He pulled his hat down. "It's going to be a cold

night. We've got to get to the railway lines. I have somewhere we can sleep there."

A couple with two children turned the corner. As they passed, the smell of warm bread came from a large paper sack the man clasped against his chest.

Magda closed her eyes. *The smell of the bread.*

The man stopped, the wife clinging to his arm and watching Magda with narrow eyes.

But he reached into the bag and tore off a large crust and gave it to Magda. His children looked up with open mouths, pale faces like moons inside a bundle of hats and scarves.

• • •

Magda and Ivan shared the bread as they walked.

"Why are you helping me, Ivan?" Magda asked through a mouthful.

He laughed.

It seemed that Ivan Rublev laughed a lot. Magda could not see so many things to laugh about.

"Just the money then?" she said.

"You helped me, Havemercy." He tore another chunk of crust. "And, besides, you're pretty enough—for a foolish country girl."

He put his strong arm over her shoulder.

In the dark she blushed. "Ivan, look."

Ahead of them, an old man shoveled snow from the steps of a church.

"I want to go in."

"Why?"

"So I can light a candle for my grandmother."

"There isn't time. We've got a long way to walk still."

"I will be quick. I promise."

He stopped his chewing. Shook his head. "Well, don't be long."

• • •

Sitting here and there along the wooden pews people bowed their heads in prayer. At the altar a priest lit the candles. He moved slowly beneath a statue of the Virgin Mary, which towered above the nave.

Magda pulled a note from the rolled bundle of money under her belt and pushed it into the collection box. She took a long, thin candle from the table, dipped it in a flame, and placed it among the others burning on a sand-filled tray.

Forgive me, Babula, for nailing your coffin with a shoe.

A priest was making his way back among the pews. Magda waylaid him in the shadows.

"Father, I want to make a confession."

"Yes." He held up a bunch of candles. "I am just replacing the candles. This way."

She followed him to a darkened alcove at the back of the church. The priest sat wearily in his seat, crossed himself. Magda knelt at the lectern. Bowed her head.

"Bless me, Father, for I have sinned."

Magda thought about what her sins had been.

"I begrudged Brunon Dudek a bag of potatoes for helping to lay out my grandmother. I took a pony from Bogdan Stopko and then I stole his money. I was jealous when parents came for the other children. I am sorry for these sins and all the sins I can't remember—"

"Is that all, girl? Is there nothing else?"

"I nailed my grandmother's coffin with a shoe."

Silence. "A shoe?"

"I was afraid of the forest spirits. I was alone and I had no hammer."

"There are no spirits in the forest. That is superstition. But why did you steal a pony?"

"To get to the next village and find help."

"You did not act in bad faith when you took the pony then?"

"No. I believe I did not."

"You must return the money you stole from this man."

"But I can't, Father. It is gone now."

"Then you must pray for forgiveness."

"There is one more thing, Father."

"Yes."

"A boy kissed me."

"Did you want him to?"

She hesitated. "I cannot stop myself thinking about it."

"Only God can look into your heart," said the priest. "Your sins are forgiven."

Magda rose. She did not feel that they were.

Ivan was waiting impatiently on the steps outside, stamping his feet. "What took you so long?"

• • •

The walk across the city continued long and cold. Ivan's destination was a scrap of land beside a disused railway siding. They ducked in through a broken fence. A dog trotted homeward on the other side of the triangle of land. The smell of smoke drifted up from a rickety chimney pipe sticking out of the roof of a rusting container. They made their way across the snow and Ivan banged on the ribbed metal doors.

"It's me."

The door swung open a crack, rusted hinges creaking. An old woman's head appeared. She looked Magda up and down.

"You can't have a girl in here! Go on!" She shook her fist at Ivan. "For shame. Go out in the snow like the dogs."

"Quiet down, Grandmother. I have some candles. She's just a friend."

Ivan pushed his way past the old woman. There was coughing. Inside, an old man lay on a bed made of pallets. In the corner a fire made from an old oil drum pumped out a ferocious heat. A stubby candle smoked on a pair of planks that sufficed for a table.

Ivan took the pack off his back and pulled out a handful of candles.

The candles from the church!

"Here," he said.

The old woman grabbed them without a word. She looked up at Magda with narrow eyes, tutting loudly.

"Let her be," Ivan said, throwing himself onto an old mattress on the other side of the makeshift room. "You can sleep here, Magda." He handed her a blanket.

"You shouldn't be out on your own with that boy. No good will come of it," said the old woman.

The old man coughed violently and she pinched his foot. Hard.

Ivan pulled his hat over his eyes. "We'll be gone tomorrow, Grandmother, so keep your thoughts to yourself."

The old woman humphed, but snuffed out the candle and said no more.

And Magda lay in the dark with her eyes wide open.

Daung. Daung. "IVAAAN!"

Magda lifted her puffy-eyed head over the blanket. The old woman was awake—feeding pathetically small sticks into the stove.

There was more impatient banging.

Ivan got up and stumbled blearily to the door. Pulling on a sweater, he opened it a crack. Weak morning light spilled across the rough planks of the floor.

One of the men from the nightclub stood out in the snow with hunched shoulders and his dark-stubbled chin stuck deep in his collar. "It's today. Valentin says you come now," the man said, shifting from side to side on his cold feet. His hands stuffed tight into the pockets of a thin leather jacket.

Ivan nodded and closed the door. "Get up, Magda. We're going."

• • •

At the edge of the wasteland a brand-new Jeep with blackened windows idled on the icy road. They followed the man as he walked across the snowy ground in unsuitable leather shoes.

Magda had never been in such a car. She climbed up inside. It was warm. Russian rap music blared. The driver sat silent in his seat.

Nazar leaned over into the back and held out a package. "Here is the delivery."

Ivan took the package. Removing his coat, he stuffed the package into one of the deep pockets sewn into the lining.

The driver turned the car in the road, the big gold rings digging into his fingers as he clutched at the gear stick.

. . .

They pulled into a high-walled yard filled with broken trucks and untidy piles of split logs. A hungry-looking Rottweiler was chained to a rusting forklift. A Turkish container lorry was parked by a dilapidated warehouse and the fat bandit was talking to the driver.

They got out. Valentin came over and put his big arm around Ivan's shoulders. He held him tight and grinned his gold-toothed grin. But it didn't look too friendly.

"What about food?" Ivan said.

Valentin snapped his fingers. Nazar went to the Jeep and came back with a plastic bag. Ivan looked inside it. Handed it to Magda. There were two large plastic bottles of water, apples, bread, and sausage.

"Not exactly a feast."

"You're not paying that sort of money, my friend. But here—" Valentin pulled a small bottle of vodka from his jacket. "A little present."

The truck driver opened the high front hood and, climbing up onto the wheel arch, he leaned over and poked a flaming rag down into the engine block.

Magda followed Ivan to the open doors at the back of the

lorry. The container was filled with bundles of fur pelts. Great big bundles the size of straw bales. They came halfway up the inside of the lorry. Ivan climbed in and pulled Magda up behind him.

"How do we know it won't get searched?"

"Don't worry, little wolf." Valentin laughed. "At least you'll be warm."

"And we go straight to London?"

"Yes. Don't let me down." He handed in a bucket with a lid. "Enjoy!"

That grinning gold-toothed face was the last thing Magda saw as the doors closed. The remains of daylight disappeared when the heavy bolts clamped shut.

Beneath her the bundles of fur were soft. She could hear Ivan breathing beside her. "Will it be dark the whole way?" she whispered.

"Yes. But at least you'll be warm."

She heard the smile in his voice

The truck started up. Chassis juddering under the bales of fur.

"It will be better if we lie down," he said. "The best we can do is sleep. It will be a long journey."

"I am afraid."

He settled down next to her. "Try not to think too much. It will be all right."

Magda closed her eyes. The darkness was too dark. If she closed her eyes, she could pretend it was not. She could pretend that she had made a choice. And that it was the right one.

• • •

At first she was nauseous with the disembodied lurching. But soon that passed and the rumbling of the engine became a comfort. It was when the jolting and rumbling stopped that she grew afraid again.

They hid then. Scrambling to the back on all fours and burying themselves in between the soft bundles of fur. But no one opened the doors.

. . .

Later, Magda dreamed. The dreams were not good. They were troubled dreams. She could not remember them when she woke, but she knew they were not good.

. . .

"Magda. Let's drink. Here." Ivan handed her the bottle of vodka. "It'll warm you up."

She put it to her lips. Tipped it back a little. The taste was harsh and bitter and burned at her throat.

"You'll get used to it. Go on."

She drank some more.

They lay on their backs, side by side.

"You remind me of a girl I knew once—" Ivan said. He thought about his friend. Anna. Warm beside him with a bottle of vodka. Just like this. A long time ago.

He closed his eyes.

"Tell me," said Magda. "Tell me about her."

Ivan turned on his side in the dark. "Sometime maybe I will. But what about you? Your mother—I suppose you know where she lives."

"I have an address."

"Why did she leave your village?"

"Like everyone. To work. She always says she's going to come back home one day, come back and buy an apartment in town. She's going to buy a good apartment for us all to live in, *and* sell Babula's cow. She did make Babula sell the cow. They had a big fight, but she did make her sell the cow in the end." Magda swigged from the bottle again, felt a lightness in her thoughts. "But I don't even remember the color of her eyes. Maybe they are green. Or brown."

"So you haven't seen her for a long time?" Ivan said.

"She comes home every summer. On a bus. She's always so tired and Babula treats her like a child and she doesn't like it, I know. But she cries when she has to go back." The alcohol flooded into her blood. Thoughts jumbled in her head.

"Well, let's hope we find her." Ivan took the bottle away.

"Ivan—" Magda coughed a little, tasted the cheap vodka at the back of her mouth. "Ivan, do you know the story of the forest spirit, Lesh-ee?"

"What?"

"Lesh-ee—"

Ivan laughed. "The spirits in the forest. Have mercy! Have mercy!"

Magda rested her hands on her stomach. Smiling in the dark. "All right. So who *are* you then?"

He rolled onto his back. "You always ask the same foolish questions."

"No, I want to know. Who are you? Tell me about your friend. Tell me about your home."

Ivan reached out for her, fumbling under the heavy pile of furs. "I am Lesh-ee. Grrrr! The spirit in the forest!"

But it wasn't funny anymore. Just like that.

She brushed him away with her hand.

Alone with her troubled thoughts.

12

On a cold dark night we are carried across the sea. To a place where men like rats from sinking ships have scurried the ropes to land.

Where gray salt waters pound the bulwarks of concrete jetties and hard gloved men hunch backs into a sea-sprayed wind. They curse with blueing and indelicate lips as their slow-moving fingers sling the freezing strops to rusting hooks.

And a battered container, lurching and swinging, is hoisted from the icy decks of a great ship. And now a new lorry that has taken possession of the load turns from the road and pulls into a snow-filled yard

This is the place. A Mountain of Glass.

Home of fifteen million spirits.

Of fifteen million mouths to be fed. And fifteen million hearts to be warmed. And fifteen million minds to be led.

Multiplying under a dark, beady lens, this great sprawling organism grows, spreading like bacillus on a dish: London.

Here Crow preaches, ragged and hungry among the crumbling darkened stucco. Spying through keyholes and hopping across the white-topped roofs where chimneys belch smoke once more into the heavy gray sky. Digesting all the while, a deficit of hope that clanks slowly from A to B and B to A, back and forth like the pendulum of some awful clock passing time.

It is here that Crow waits.

And watches.

And keeps its privy counsel.

. . .

Magda felt that she was back in her bed in Morochov. Babula was pressing her hand with cool, old fingers. Babula, mopping her brow. The old woman leaned close, Magda could feel the breath on her cheek. There were voices out on the porch. It was the priest. And the Dudek brothers.

Magda could hear them talking.

It was as if she were waking from a dream.

Babula seemed to be leaning on her in the cool dark of the bedroom. It was difficult to breathe.

Babula. Babula, you are so heavy.

She could hear the priest in the room. She tried to open her eyes.

She has been a very bad girl, Father.

Yes, she has.

I told her not to listen to the spirits in the forest, said Brunon Dudek, standing at the foot of the bed. *We'll help lay her out, Agnieszka.*

A bag of potatoes is all you're getting, Brunon Dudek.

Magda could feel hands pinching under the bedclothes: the cold hands of the spirits from the forest.

Have you dug her grave, Agnieszka?

Under the apple trees, Father. Nail the coffin shut with your shoe.

Magda tried to raise her head as she was lifted from the bed. Was she dying? She did not want to die. She did not want to be buried under the apple trees. She grabbed for the blankets.

No! Don't let them take me, Ivan.

But they were carrying her into the garden. The light was bright. She tried to open her eyes.

I don't want to be buried under the apple trees!

The priest laughed. The Dudek brothers laughed.

Ivan. Help me!

The light grew stronger. It was so bright.

Don't bury me!

. . .

"Wake up! It's just a dream. Have some water." Ivan opened the bottle of water and found Magda's hand.

He knew they had crossed the sea while Magda had slept. The engine had stopped but the lurching had gotten worse.

Magda let a little of the cold water trickle onto her tongue and down her throat, and lay back on the bundles of fur.

"Just rest, Magda. We will be in London soon."

And what will there be when they open the doors? she thought. The opening of the doors meant that tomorrow would come at last. The world would come back with the light. *You do not know where you are going. What will happen. What you will find.*

She felt like the dog, Azor, waiting in the snow, watching the world disappear. Everything hurt. Her knees throbbed. A dull thumping ache behind her eyes. Ivan was close beside her. It comforted her a little.

The container lurched with a loud bang and was still.

. . .

"Hey! You! Truck of finished pelt need unloading. And your friend."

The short Russian who issued this command rubbed his hands together in the cold. He was wearing a long fur coat that made him look even shorter.

A man stood up from bending over the salty rawhides he had been heaving onto a conveyor belt.

"Oy mate!" he shouted at his friend, whose head and arms were hidden inside a rinsing drum.

"Mate!" he shouted again above the din of the machines.

The man pulled his head out. Mouthed a *What?*

The first man pointed out through the hanging plastic sheeting at the open door of the warehouse. "We've got to unload a truck."

The other man slammed the red plastic power button with the palm of his hand and the conveyor ground to a halt. "I'm effing freezing. What time is it?"

"Three-ish."

The two stood side by side at a metal sink, washing their bloody hands. Hung their aprons on hooks on the wall.

"Is it a big load?"

His friend peered through the plastic sheeting into the yard.

"Looks like it."

They pulled on their hats and jackets and stepped outside. The lorry had parked in the unloading bay.

The Russian saw them and put up his hand. "Wait!" he barked.

"What the bleeding hell—?" The man stamped his feet. "I'm freezing my nuts off out here! What's he doing?"

"Dunno."

Two coat-bundled figures stumbled along the wall of the yard toward the open road.

"Look!"

The Russian came striding back across the snow. "What you look at? Get on with it!" And he scuttled back inside the warehouse.

The man nudged his friend and pointed. "That was illegals in the truck."

"Not our problem, mate," said his friend, and they adjusted their hats, and with heads low they stomped out into the yard.

13

The doors of the container opened. Magda turned her head to the light, blinked, shielded her eyes with her hand.

There was a man wearing a fur coat.

He seemed to be shouting at them. "You go now. You cannot stay."

"We have to get out, Magda," Ivan said. "Give me your mother's address."

"Get her out. You have to go," the man shouted.

Magda pulled her mother's address from the pocket of her coat.

"We need to find this place—"

The Russian grabbed the scrap of paper and looked at it. "Down road. Station. You go train to Hampstead Heath."

They scrambled down from the bales of fur and jumped onto the concrete floor of an open shed. Magda stood unsteadily on her legs. Blinked in the light. Ivan talked to the Russian in the fur coat.

He looked paler than she remembered. He turned and smiled at her. It wasn't the same face that had laughed at her over the fire in the forest. Or the face in the shadows of the nighttime in

Krakow. Or the face she had imagined in the darkness. But still smiling. He took an envelope from the Russian.

She leaned against the doors of the container. The back of her neck still throbbed.

"I need to sit down."

"We have to leave this place. I'll find somewhere to rest. I promise. Here, lean on me."

Magda let her weight fall on Ivan's shoulder. He helped her along the side of the container. Saw two men staring at them from the warehouse.

"Hurry, Magda. We must get away from here."

Out on the road the snow was plowed into dirty heaps along the pavement. With approaching dusk, the sky was growing dingy between the rooftops. A small electric car whirred slowly along the icy white. It disappeared around a corner between the shabby warehouses.

They found a dark, narrow alleyway that led to nowhere, and sat in the snow behind some large plastic bins. She managed a smile. "This is London, Ivan. It doesn't seem much better than Krakow, does it?"

"We have to get to the train station. The Russian told me it is not far. It's nearly dark. That will give us some cover."

Magda leaned back against the wall with her coat pulled close around her, hands tucked under her arms.

They were here. In London. England.

Against all the odds.

And when she found Mama the world would fall back into place.

Her hand crept inside her pocket to the carefully folded paper there. Mama's address.

Mama. At last.

. . .

"Yalla! Yalla!"

Ivan jumped up and peered around the corner of the alleyway.

"What is it?" She crept up beside him.

Farther up the road, a dingy electric light glanced across the sidewalk from the door of a liquor store. In front of the grilled windows a group of boys hung around in the snow, drinking from unmarked bottles—accompanied by a ragtag group of stocky, square-snouted dogs, bristling like loaded weapons.

Another group of youths straggled out of a side street. "I ain't blettin' doin' it, blud. Give me your phone—"

A dog snarled. The drinking boys stepped out from their street-side barracks.

"Yalla, yalla! Listen to dis, chungdys! CDB are takin' ova Camden bluds!"

They got their response, with gestures crude: "No man! TMS are pinchin' ova Camden 'n soon takin' ova London. We got dogz blud, you feel me? They gonna rip you up like shankin'!"

Shouting from along the street. The sound of breaking glass. A bottle smashed against a wall.

Snarling and barking.

Bellowing.

Padding footfalls.

"—don't joke no more. Faisal killed Gek but don't think you gonna get away wid dat medevil shit."

Dull, thick sounds of boots on ice. More barking.

"If you lot mediboys come try another thing like dat. Chungdy. This me, ova here."

Running feet. Slathering, teeth snapping.

"—don't come frontline Camden sans invite, coz we is Camden-DogBoyz and we'll terrorize you marginuls—"

Running. Shouting. "They got him! They blettin' got Shaddy, bludz!"

Footsteps stumped toward the alleyway.

A flailing blur of legs, and dogs with flattened ears jumping and snapping. And then they were past. Braying in the dark.

"Quick," said Ivan.

Magda followed him out onto the street, skirting along in the shadows of the buildings, broken bottles crunching underfoot. They ducked down a side road. They pulled up for a second against the wall, Magda's breath hammering in her throat.

"Magda. You all right?"

"What happened?"

"This is not a good part of the city," Ivan said, and leaned breathless against the wall beside her. "That's all. I think we're safe now."

"But why were they fighting?"

"People always fight over scraps." He pushed himself up. "Come on, we need to keep going."

Magda stumbled after him in her heavy coat, the bag slapping on her back as they picked up the pace once more.

Soon they came to a wide road. Cars drove slowly on the ice. Ivan stopped. "There. It's down there. Where the man said." Ivan pointed across the road to an open, steaming hole on the darkening street. "The train station."

Magda followed him as he crossed the road at a fast clip, head down, looking over his shoulder from time to time, heading for the damp stairway sucking streams of people from the cold streets into the dimness.

Below ground, all was noise and gloom. The air stale from a thousand breaths. Muffled in large coats, people trudged by in lines. Some haggled over pathetic collections of old boots and tawdry goods that had been laid out on blankets on the ground. And in dark corners the homeless and desperate crouched, begging cigarettes from nervous characters who preyed in the shadows of stairwells and broken lifts.

By a battered table, a woman with flaking nail varnish stood beside a steaming coffee urn. She saw two tired-looking kids edging nervously through the crowds.

"Quid fer a cup-a-coffee," she shouted. "Quid fer a cup-a-coffee. You want a nice cup-a-coffee?" She beckoned to them. "Only a quid."

Magda looked at Ivan, but he shook his head.

The woman studied their faces. "You look like you need a bit of luck, don't you, my loves. Still, it ain't my stall so I can't give you a coffee. But cheer up"—she leaned close—"the guard's gone for a fag, so you can jump the gates if you're quick." She winked.

Magda translated for Ivan, and they pushed across the crowded ticket hall and vaulted over the gates. They made their way along the dingy tunnels. Down the silent escalators, wide-eyed, past women selling hot rice in newspaper cones. Along the cold, tiled passageways, and through the arches to the platform.

Two policemen strode through the crowd, guns in their belts.

Ivan hung back against the wall.

A train clanked in from the dark of the tunnel. Squealed to a halt. Doors opened. People spilled out onto the platform.

They jumped into the carriage. Found themselves stuck against the dirty glass as the bodies crammed in. Packed like chickens in a crate.

The policemen drew nearer.

"Mind the gap. Stand clear of the doors," said an automated voice. The doors slid shut and the train lurched forward into the dark tunnel.

No one talked or moved—just rocked en masse as the train bumped along the tracks with a grating and a clunking and the flashing of lights.

"Do you know where we are going?" Magda whispered.

"Yes. Hampstead Heath. That is what the Russian said."

. . .

Like a gannet, the train disgorged its gutful.

A man—it does not matter what his name is—trudged from the bowels of the station up to the cold street above, shoved along shoulder to shoulder with the miserable dull-coated backs of the others.

The lucky ones.

He was thinking of his supper perhaps, and trying to remember that things hadn't always been like this.

It's just a blip. We'll get over it. That's what they said to begin with—and now a million people were jumping out of the woodwork telling you it was solar cycles or a new Ice Age or goddamn Armageddon.

The stations struggled to keep trains running. Always crowded. Always slow. But warmer than the street. As soon as the first frosts cut at the windows, every homeless person headed underground. And no one looked at the woman with arms outstretched at the top of the stairs. He too stepped around her. *You can't help everyone.* Sometimes it was hard enough to help yourself.

Up on the street the other workers fanned across the icy road, drawing out umbrellas as wet snow began to fall from the orange-domed London night sky.

Struggling with his own umbrella, he caught sight of a girl, face wet with snow, darting between the passengers, holding out a piece of paper. Not much older than his daughter. An illegal, by the looks of her.

God knows where these people came from. Didn't they know it wasn't any better here?

• • •

Like a moth in the rain, Magda dodged between the bent backs and go-away eyes outside the train station.

Snowflakes wet the paper in her hand.

She saw a man glancing up as he began to open his umbrella. She caught his eye and hurried toward him.

"I try to find this address?"

He did not look away. He peered down at Babula's faded handwriting and pointed across the road. "Along the heath, one of the roads on the left, I think." Then, with the quick, embarrassed smile of impromptu charity and a mumbled "good luck," he flicked up his umbrella and went on his way.

• • •

It was quiet when Magda and Ivan got away from the bustling train station. Behind partly boarded-up railings on the other side of the road, the overgrown bushes and trees of Hampstead Heath leaned their shaggy silhouettes. Lone tire tracks, perfect as tram lines, trailed in the snow toward the end of the road. A street light flickered, buzzed, and went out.

They walked along, feet falling weary on the fresh snow that still dropped from above.

Magda thought constantly of her mother. So near now.

To tell Mama that Babula had gone? How would that be? She could remember the crying behind the shutters. *What if Mama cried again? There is no Babula to tell you to go outside, even though you are too old to play.*

The wind gathered, a wild sighing from the dark woodland stretching out across the heath. A panic fluttered within her. Eating her cold insides. For there was another question she had not let herself ask before, and still she pushed it away.

What if she's not there. What then?

She looked again at the address in her hand.

This was the road.

The street was gated—six-foot-high railings topped with razor wire. She peered in at the circular drive of tall, detached townhouses. There were lights behind heavily curtained windows.

This is where Mama lives?

A dim light emanated from behind the steamy window of a guard's hut. Inside it, the shadow of a seated man—chin resting on his chest.

Ivan knocked on the window. The guard stirred and opened his eyes.

"What shall I say?" she whispered.

"Tell him your mother works here."

The guard caught sight of the two hooded faces at his window. He frowned.

"I look for my mother," Magda said loudly through the glass.

With a general air of wariness the man slid the window open a crack. "And?" he said in Polish.

"My mother, she works here." Magda held up the address. Pushed the scrap of paper toward the opening.

"*Dayą.*" The man grabbed it with clumsy fingers. Yawned as he read it. He looked back at her blankly.

"Please," she said.

"*Czekają!*" He thrust the paper back through the window, closed it, and got up. He came out behind the fence and unlocked the gates. Pushing them open, he glanced down the deserted street. "I'll give you five minutes. But I'm watching you." He let them in. "It's the fourth house on the left."

Magda padded along the pavement, looked at the address on her piece of paper, and back to the number on the door of the house.

No. 7

A holly bush arched over the front garden, sharp leaves perfect with snow. Curtains were drawn at the tall windows, but light spilled from behind them.

She took a deep breath and climbed the wide stone steps.

Her hand wavered.

And with one nervous glance at the guard eyeing her from his hut, and one at Ivan waiting shiftily on the pavement, she knocked.

Noises from inside. Footsteps.

A clinking of locks.

From behind a chain, the door opened a crack.

"Yes?" A woman's face appeared. She looked nervously at Ivan, then down the street. "Who are you?" she asked.

"Is Maria Krol here?" Magda said.

"What?"

"Maria Krol."

The woman pushed the door shut. They heard her calling out: "Mike." There were loud footfalls on a staircase. Whispering behind the door: *Someone looking for Maria.*

The chain was taken off and a man came out, hands in the

pockets of his trousers. He glanced along the road and raised a hand at the guard, turned back to Magda. "Can I help?"

"I am looking for Maria Krol," Magda said.

"And?"

"I am daughter. I come from Poland."

"Her daughter?"

"Yes."

"Why've you come *here*?"

"Her telephone is dead. I only have your address."

"She doesn't work for us anymore."

"What is it, Mike?" The man's wife had come out onto the steps behind him.

"Maria's daughter."

"When she leave?" Magda said. Panic thrashing away inside her. "When?"

"A month ago."

"One month? But—it cannot be possible?"

"Well, it's a fact." The man looked faintly annoyed.

"Where she go?" Magda said.

"I don't know. Poland, I guess."

The lights in the hallway suddenly went out.

"Dad!" came a shout from inside. There was a pattering of footsteps. A small girl in pajamas came out. She was holding a torch and shone it in Magda's face.

"Stop that, Jo," said the woman.

"But we're in the middle of a game—"

"Come on, it's freezing." The woman pulled the child back

inside. "You can't stand outside in your jim-jams. I'll put the generator on, Mike."

They turned, the torch wavering in the dark hallway.

"How can I find her?" Magda said.

"I don't know. Sorry. Look. I really can't help you—"

The lights in the house came back on at the faint rumbling of a generator somewhere deep inside.

There was a clanging of the gates at the end of the road and a small car pulled in and passed slowly by. Inside the car, a woman's pale face turned momentarily toward the two strangely dressed figures outside No. 7.

The man glanced down the road again. "Look, you've really got to go now," he said. And with a half-sorry shrug he stepped back inside his house and closed the door.

Just like that.

Magda stood, frozen, on the steps.

"He has said she is not there?" Ivan asked.

But Magda did not hear him. She turned and looked along the darkened row of houses. Clear as a cold cloudless day. It was as if she were waking from a dream. She had been so foolish. Foolish from the start. A foolish country girl—

"We have to go," Ivan said. "Maybe they will call the police."

"Where, Ivan?" she said quietly. "Where?"

14

A hungry fox padded across the snow under the avenue of bare lime trees on Hampstead Heath.

It stopped.

Smelled the air.

Something had passed.

Dropping its head, the fox trotted nervously on, its long russet back disappearing under a bank of brambles on the other side of the track.

Slowly filling with snow, human footprints led away from the fence and under the trees. The footprints veered from the path— the trampled marks suggesting a moment of indecision. They trailed into the thicket, snow brushed from fallen branches marking their going. Far off, muffled by the trees, came the rising-falling wail of a police car making its way through the London night.

• • •

Magda stopped. They had come in thick among the undergrowth, branches tangled against the night sky.

"Why didn't she find a way to tell me, Ivan?"

The few lit windows of inhabited buildings had melted away behind them. Under the trees the soft darkness enveloped them.

"It won't help thinking about that now," he said. "Things don't always turn out like you want them." He pulled his hat down low. "Stay close and keep quiet. We'll find somewhere to make a fire at least. Away from the road. We can get warm. Think what to do next."

She clung to his side. Every biting footstep seemed louder than the last. The things she had imagined, things from before, they had been left behind in Morochov. *Why had Mama left London?* It was as if nothing made sense anymore: the things that tied her to herself, even those ropes were fraying, and the threads were snapping.

Little bits of good and simple truth had fallen away, even as the priest had said his words over Babula's coffin. And then with every step along the river, and calling out in the dark of the forest. Nothing had been gained with stealing Stopko's money or remembering the blood of his pony falling on the snow.

She shook herself. Mama must be trying to get back home. And now she too must do the same. *But back to where? And how?*

Ahead of her, Ivan gestured with his hand. Put his finger to his lips. She bent double and crouched close beside him. He battled his way under a holly bush and she followed. Down below them through the trees was a frozen lake. The smell of smoke drifted to them on the chilled air. Human voices rang out.

With sparks spitting high and popping out in the smoky black, a large, untidy bonfire was burning at the water's edge. The leaping flames glowed orange on the sparkling white that stretched out into the darkness beyond. Two young men sat beside the fire in an upturned wheelbarrow, drinking from a bottle.

And out on the ice, beyond the flames, was a great gaggle of men. Someone turned to light a cigarette, a concentrated face caught in the light of a match.

The crowd jostled. A stocky figure in a bearskin hat stood on a crate, shoulders raised above the throng: an angry conductor with a snarling grin across his face. "Fifty-seven, fifty-eight, fifty-nine— Ten minutes in the water!" His hand beat time as he peered into the melee: "Well done, lads!" he shouted. "But my money's on Fat Ferguson!"

The raucous shouting of the excited men rose up.

"One down!" the ringmaster shouted. "Haul him out."

"What is it?" Magda whispered.

The crowd parted and made way as something was dragged between them.

A wet, naked man. His body shaking like a landed fish. The youths from the fire double-timed it over with the barrow and bundled the frozen body into blankets; wheeled him with bare feet dangling and bouncing over to the warmth of the fire.

And Magda saw then—behind the parted legs—that a hole had been cut in the ice. The water a dark stain on the white. And in the water. Other men. Grease-smeared heads bowed in painful concentration. Holding themselves with elbows back against the jagged edge, clutching at a rope they could no longer feel in their frozen-numb fingers.

The shouting rose again.

"Twenty-five, twenty-six, twenty-seven—"

"The Scot's out! Just Ferguson and the Chinaman left!"

The crowd roared in laughter.

There was a splash. Another body, thin and brown, dragged out of the water and wheeled away to the fireside.

The ringmaster urging on the crowd of onlookers. "Odds on. Twelve minutes on Ferguson. Hold in there, lad. Fifty-six, fifty-seven, fifty-eight, fifty-nine. Thirteen minutes! Get him out!"

There was a huge cheer. Men crowded around waving bits of paper.

"I think they are betting on how long the men can stay in the water," whispered Ivan.

The ringmaster's voice boomed again. "Last round. Which one of you lads is gonna try their toes! Fifty quid a drop and another hundred if you win."

A Jeep crawled under the trees with headlights off. Two men got out. Swaggered to the group on the ice. The ringmaster stepped away from the crowd and handed over the takings.

• • •

"See over there. We can double back on ourselves without anyone noticing." Ivan pointed to the far side of the lake.

They slunk back under the trees, and the voices of the men on the ice faded behind them. Clambering up a bank, they arrived at a pathway.

"We'll freeze out here," Magda said. "Where are we going to—"

But Ivan was staring down at the edge of the track. The wind rattled the spidery branches above them.

"What?"

He gestured down underneath the trees. There was a dark patch on the snow. "There's been a fire here." His voice was low. "And not long ago. We're not alone."

Magda glanced about nervously. Saw a wooden board on posts. "Look. There's a sign." She found the box of matches. Pulling off her gloves, she struck one, shielded the flame with her hand, and held it up. It was a map of the park. Still readable.

"We're here." She pointed to the weather-faded picture. They studied it together. The match burnt to her fingers. She shook it and threw it to the ground. Pulled out another. "There. The path goes that way toward the road. But there are houses. In the park. Look. To the east of us. *Vale of Health*," she said, reading the words.

She looked at the side of Ivan's face in the flickering light. "Shall we go there?"

"Yes. We might find somewhere out of the snow. It will be better."

• • •

A gap in the thicket led down a narrow path between the bushes. A swathe of snow carpeted a treeless clearing, and down in the hollow a low stand of bare hawthorn fringed a small body of frozen water. At the end of the clearing a small deer bounded with three leaps into the undergrowth.

They trod silently along a narrow path. And then, almost in an instant, they stepped out onto a crescent of snow at the water's edge. At their feet, a small abandoned dinghy attached to a taut, frost-rimed rope was entombed in the frozen water.

The night clouds thinned; the moon glowing behind them cast

a dull gleam on the iced pond. It was longer than it was wide—oval almost—surrounded on all sides by trees and bushes.

Way back from the water's edge the slab of a building rose up above bare hazel brushwood. Dark windows glowered from its tall, pale facade.

"What's that?"

"Where?"

Magda looked up at the building.

"I'm sure I saw a light."

Ivan beckoned with his hand. "Just keep your eyes open."

They skirted along the wall of the building and came out onto a road. It was strange. A single street of houses in the middle of the park. Drifts of snow were piled against doorways. Nothing moved. There was not a light to be seen. Nor a sound to be heard.

The single roadway disappeared under the trees. Ivan turned and looked back the way they had come. "This place is deserted. Why?"

Magda sat down in the snow. "We need to find somewhere to sleep. I'm tired."

"We can sleep here. Break into a house."

"What about going back to the train station?"

"No. This is better." He put out his hand to pull her up.

Perhaps it was then. A rope thrown down into the well. She looked up at him. How would she know what awaited her if she climbed to the top of it? But his hand felt strong and sure and she let it pull her up. In any case, she was too tired to argue.

And at the end of the row of abandoned houses was one low

cottage on its own. Its windows were boarded up. And to the side of it was a wooden gate set in a high brick wall. They squeezed through into a courtyard at the back of the house. A lean-to shed abutted the back wall. Above it was a shuttered window under the eaves of the house.

"Maybe there is someone here," Magda whispered.

"I don't think so." Ivan handed her his pack and pulled himself up on a water butt under the eaves. He climbed onto the roof and inched his way across the deep snow that quilted the tiles, edging carefully on all fours toward the window.

Grabbing the window frame with one hand for balance, he gave a hard pull and with a loud clatter the shutters came open.

"Be careful," she whispered up at him.

He turned his face away and elbowed the windowpane. The glass shattered loudly. He balanced there. Listening. Then reached a hand in and opened the latch.

Magda watched as he slithered headfirst through the opening, his boots disappearing into the darkness. She heard the thump as he landed on the floor inside.

"Ivan—" she called up nervously.

His head appeared. "The matches."

She fumbled in her pocket. Found the box of matches. Threw them up. She heard a strike. The sound of his feet.

"Ivan—"

Nothing.

"Ivan—"

"Wait, I'll open the door." A brief glow from a lit match.

She leaned against the wall of the shed. Closed her eyes. Hunger gnawed and rumbled in her guts. She felt a tiredness that was almost painful, blotting out the panic.

How will you ever get back to what was before?

That small glimmer of hope was fading so fast that she felt she would fall over right there.

You are like an animal—hiding in the dark of this strange place.

There was the sound of unlatching. The turning of locks in the door at the back of the house.

And there Ivan stood. Match in hand.

Maybe it had begun in the forest. Stirring his porridge. But then she had thought him so arrogant and rude. And he had stolen her food. Half her food. Laughed at her.

An ache was growing like a painful tooth.

She had never felt such a thing before.

Ivan stepped out of the doorway, smiling.

"Come on. It's empty."

15

It was dark and silent in the house. On the dusty windowsill were two half-burnt candles. He lit one. It spat and guttered alight, and he cracked it off the windowsill and held it up. There were cupboards along the wall. A table and two chairs. A pan left lying on the stove.

In a small room at the front, a heavy curtain hung at the boarded front door. Ivan lifted it. The door was bolted from the inside and locked tight. He let the curtain fall.

They climbed a narrow stair, hands against the walls, the candle casting shadows beneath their feet.

"What's up here?" Magda whispered.

"Just empty rooms."

Magda peered around the door of a bathroom and Ivan pulled the shutter closed, his feet crunching on the broken glass that had fallen onto the tiles.

Under the sloping eaves at the front of the cottage was a room with a bed. Magda sat on the bare mattress with a heavy sigh. "Do you think we're safe here?"

"Yes. I will light a fire," Ivan said. "See if there's food." He gave her the candle—dripping wax and sticking it on the small table beside the bed.

"I won't be far. Give me your pack." She pulled it off her shoulder and her head sank onto the mattress. She heard his feet padding downstairs. His hand tapping the wall in the darkness. The candle fluttered. She breathed heavily in the cold, still air.

And closed her eyes.

But there was a picture inside her head and Ivan filled it.

All the ways he moved. The stride of his legs as he walked into the light of the fire in the forest. His angular hands tearing at the bread outside the church in Krakow. His cheek turning as he laughed at her.

• • •

Downstairs, Ivan lit the other candle from the windowsill.

He would need to find sticks to light a fire. Maybe in the shed outside.

He turned the handle on the back door. The latch clicked open and the snowy courtyard gleamed in the moonlight. He breathed in the freshness of the cold air. It had stopped snowing.

Far off in the woods came a screeching, barking sound.

It wasn't human.

An animal? The small deer they had seen maybe.

The shed smelled of oil. He made out a pile of sticks and branches on the floor. The glint of a small axe hanging on the wall. He lifted the axe, bundled some sticks under his arm, and made his way back to the house.

He took the pan from the kitchen and filled it with snow from the back step. He locked the door. Tugged at the handle to be sure.

Crouching over the hearth, he scrunched some paper in the grate, laid the twigs, and struck a match to the wigwam of twigs. Wisping smoke trails disappeared up the chimney. Gently he added the broken branches. The fire grew stronger. He split a log on the floor of the room. Stared at the flames. Fanned the embers every now and then. Felt the warmth in his hands.

In the kitchen he found a couple of rusting tins of tomatoes at the back of a cupboard.

Clutching a can, he came back and sat cross-legged by the fire, laid more logs on the flames, balanced the pan of snow among them, and prized open the tin with his knife.

This was a good place to stay. If they could get more food. He stabbed his knife into a whole plum tomato and stuffed it dripping into his mouth.

A deer maybe. Set a trap.

He ate slowly. Enjoying the growing warmth. And he thought about old friends.

Anna.

He stabbed another tomato.

He remembered the first time he had seen her. Standing in line for the sinks with the other children. Her thin face, bold under dark hair, hair cropped short against lice. Anna. The only one to help him. Holding his small hand, wiping his tears away. "Forget yesterday. You've only got yourself here," she had said.

Even then, when they were both children, she had been arrogant with knowing things and smarter than a rat. Anna showed him how to get a bit more food, a better blanket. Who to avoid, when to be counted. You had few friends in Children's Home Number Thirty-Nine. She helped him learn. Fast.

At breakfast they would drink the watered milk. "Don't eat. We're going to run away today," she'd say. And they'd hide the bread in their pockets. Slip out of a bathroom window. It was high and their thin knees scraped on the concrete wall.

But then they were free. And they would laugh together and stake out in a forgotten-looking place. By the railway lines perhaps. Away from where the drunks loitered.

And Anna showed Ivan the way to tie a snare with old wire—because she had come from the countryside—that's all she said about it. Never more. And they would place the scrap of food they had saved from breakfast, and lay it out to catch a bird.

It was good when you never ate anything better than chicken-feet and hard bread. They would roast it over their fire, laughing, talking, falling asleep with greasy hands and bony ribs.

But they were always caught. Always sent back.

One time Anna said: "Let's not go back, Ivan. Ever."

And they didn't.

They grew up quickly on the streets, learned how to avoid the police, to scavenge for food, to stamp on the drunkards' toes and huddle together in out-of-the-way places. Ivan grew tall and strong. Anna's hair grew long at last. Their first kiss by the train station. Ivan had felt his strength when he pulled her toward him that first time. Anna laughed and kissed him ten times on his face afterward.

"We will go to England. It is better there. That is what they say. We just need money. Maybe America one day," she said, smiling her thin-lipped smile inside the photo booth.

Kaflash!

"Two for you, two for me," she said, tearing the sheet in half. "I've got bad teeth, haven't I?" She laughed again. Anna always laughed.

"Why do I need two pictures?" he had asked her.

"For the passport, stupid. You need a passport to go to America."

"But we can't both be in it."

"We'll do it again. That one's just so you don't ever forget me!"

They learned to slip and slide. To dream.

They always needed more money. But in the winter they always spent all they had saved on food and keeping warm.

And Anna learned to dream with a bottle of vodka. More than she liked to dream with Ivan. Her dreams slipped away under the bridge. Men came. She went with them.

And that was that.

Ivan found other ways to get by.

• • •

The snow melted in the pan. He pulled off his coat. Naked to the waist, he began to wash. Splashing the water onto his face. Rivulets ran down his chest and he wiped at them with his shirt.

Yes, a deer would be good.

Then he'd think how to get to Gulbekhian. That was the plan. Deliver the passports. Go back. Get the money. East. That's what

Valentin had said. The money's all going east. Maybe he would find Anna again.

Maybe not.

Even Ivan had fettered dreams.

· · ·

He reached out a lean, bare arm. Picked up a strong stick. He held it against his leg and whittled away at the end with his knife. Honing a sharp point. He would need something to kill the deer if he snared it.

And Magda?

The shavings fell on the hearth.

She had pushed him away. Kicked at him when he'd tried to kiss her. He smiled to himself.

He wasn't used to that.

Like Valentin had said—there were a million girls. There was something about her face though, something that made him remember. From before.

He started.

There was movement above. The faint glow from a candle falling on the stairs. The tread of feet.

Magda came down and stepped blearily to the fire.

"How long have I been sleeping?" She put her hands out to the warmth. "It's so good." She stood a little longer. "The fire, I mean."

He looked at her then. Her long hair a mess. The rounded cheekbones and the look of her, something sharp and soft all at once. Something capable he recognized. Something that smelled familiar.

"I found some food," he said. "Here."

She crouched down beside him and picked out a tomato. Began unlacing her boots. "It hasn't turned out so well, has it?"

Her mouth. That was it. Like fruit that was hanging out of reach. Ivan was sure he could climb the tree.

"Maybe you could try praying." He smiled. "You like all that."

She stopped and looked at him. Put her boots beside the fire.

"I never really thought about it," she said. "I mean, really."

"Thought about what?"

She pulled off her damp socks and laid them on the hearth, wrapped her arms about her legs. Stared into the flames. "All that."

Ivan pushed at the embers with the stick. "We need to find new clothes."

"I mean, what have we done to deserve this . . . ?" She rested her head on her knees.

"Deserve? Your god and his punishments live in churches," Ivan said. "It's just country talk. We need to get clean and look like the other people so the police don't notice us. Think what to do."

"It isn't just in churches, Ivan."

"Well, I haven't heard of it anywhere else. And, anyway, if your god's not just in churches, why are you wondering? It's stupid."

"I don't know anymore. It all seemed simple before."

"First we need to get clothes and food."

She turned her head toward him. "Maybe my mother is trying to find me."

"I don't think so."

"Why?"

"Because she thinks you are still at home with your grandmother." He looked away. Hacked with his knife. "Anyway, the world isn't the way you think it is. We must go to Liverpool. Get the money."

She rested her chin on her knees again and stared into the fire, nudged her boot along the slate of the hearth with her bare toes. "Ivan—"

He looked at her. "What?"

"You—"

But her words came out so small.

She wanted them to sound different.

Her lips clamped shut. Her heart thumped loud in her chest.

The fire crackled some more.

And then Ivan laughed. "So—" He put his arm over her shoulder. "You want to kiss me now?"

She pushed him away, her face red.

"It's not funny!" Magda cried.

He leaned over. "Yes it is. Come on, give me a kiss, country girl."

"Get off!" She pushed at him.

He pulled away. Laughed again.

"Everything's funny to you, Ivan. Everything." She was angry. So suddenly.

"No, not everything—"

"You're always laughing at me—"

"You don't know me, Magda."

"So why did you bring me here? To laugh at my misfortune?"

"You wanted to come..."

"That's all?"

What *could* he say? He couldn't tell her about her mouth like a fruit, and the look of her face, and the way she reminded him of someone else.

"I needed to get to England," he said. "You had money."

Magda let out a cry. Got up on her knees. A fury inside her. "You could have taken it. Just taken it!" She lashed out with her fists. "You lied! Why did you bring me here?"

Ivan dropped the knife, shielding his head from the blows, and grabbed at her wrists. "Lie? About what? Stop!"

She twisted in his grip, her face distorted. "You're a liar! You're no good!"

"I did not lie to you."

"I wish you had stolen the money. It would have been better than this."

"Stop now!" He fought her twisting hands.

"You're a liar!"

"STOP!"

His loudness stamped a calm in the storm.

Her breaths rose and fell in angry bursts.

"You wanted to come, Magda. And I was helping you. Why are you being like this?"

She turned her face away.

"And I'm not laughing at your misfortune. I'm sorry," he said.

"Sorry for what?" The words caught in her throat.

"For how it has happened," he said. "Sorry your mother was not there."

"And you helped me because of the money?"

"The money is not everything."

"I gave you Stopko's money. I came with you. Now I've got nothing."

"You've got me—"

She turned away from him. "I wish I had stayed at home."

"Sleep," he said. "It is better. We'll talk tomorrow."

He put a log on the fire.

But Magda did not sleep. She was aware of his occasional shifting as he sat beside her.

"Everything will be all right," he said softly. "Trust me."

She turned and saw his shadowed face, halved by the firelight. Eyes dark and glassy, tiny pinpricks in the flickering light.

"I did trust you, Ivan," she said. "But you just keep yourself closed, like a book."

"Why are you so interested in me?"

"Because I don't know anything about you. Who you are. Where you come from—"

He stared at the fire. "My mother came to Poland with me in her belly. She was very young then. Her name was Luba Rublev. She married a man—Pokova—and had three other children with him. This man Pokova, he was always drunk. And angry. He beat me, and he beat my mother and sometimes he beat his own children too. I don't remember much else, except that."

"And your mother?"

Ivan tried to remember his mother.

There were her hands. That time when he'd found a bird fallen from its nest in the eaves.

"Leave it," she said. "You can't help it."

"We could put it in a box."

"No. Some things are best left to take their own chances."

"Please, Mama."

He carried it inside. And she had helped him fill a little box. He remembered her hands poking about and the grass scratching at the cardboard as she rounded a hollow.

And *him,* drunk in the corner, laughing. "Yaagh. It'll be deadinthemornin'."

. . .

Ivan leaned forward and poked about in the fire. "My mother came from a town in the Ukraine. Sometimes she would go home to visit her parents there. She took me across the border. Said I would see my grandmother. When we got off the bus, she left me by the side of a street. She said she'd come back. I waited. And waited.

"It was winter. I was cold. I hid by the bus station. I cried. But no one came. After two days I went back to the street because I was hungry and cold. And the police got me and took me to the Children's Home."

"How old were you?"

"Six."

"And you're running away from that?"

"I want to be something on this earth, Magda. I don't want to sit and become nothing."

Magda closed her eyes. "You won't become something just by running away."

"What do you know?" he said.

Magda looked at the side of his face. "And, anyway, how are you going to leave something on the earth if you don't sit still?"

Ivan rubbed at his cheek. "Those are just pretty words, Magda. In the real world it is money that talks." He lay down on the floor beside her and pulled the blanket over his shoulders. "You think you understand me now?"

They were silent for a moment.

"What will I do if I can't find my mother back home?"

"You think you have a home still?" he said.

She did not reply.

"I like you, Magda. I will help you." He put his arm over her and she lay like that with the weight of it across her stomach, rising and falling with her breaths.

"In my village," she said, "there was a man. Brunon Dudek. For him, our village was the only place in the world. He didn't want anything more."

Ivan felt Magda's heartbeat quicken.

What more was there to know about a person than the lost things that made them whole?

And tomorrow would wind around like always. With something new to lose and maybe something new to gain.

That is how he had learned to think.

Weighing it up. Balancing the scales for tomorrow. Hoping for something cast and heavy that clunked heavily to earth and stayed there. He felt her body under his arm. And it felt good right then.

"You're not alone, Magda."

She could feel his breath on her cheek.

She could feel the warmth.

She felt his fingers creep around her waist.

"You have to believe that you will find the thing you are looking for," he said.

Her heart beat a thousand drumbeats.

"Why can't it be the things that were before?" she whispered.

"Why can't it just be here? Tonight, Magda?"

Maybe he was right.

"When I saw you—" he said.

"In the forest?"

"No. I was on the hill, laughing at you. You looked like an ant in a puddle down on the road in the snow with your pony and your dog. I saw you looking back the way you had come. You could have turned around then and gone home to your village. You had not come so far. But you didn't turn back.

"I thought you were a foolish country girl"—he brushed the hair from her cheek—"but you did not turn back—"

She remembered herself then, by the river in Morochov. Sitting on the grass in the sun. In the village, the barking of a dog. Men coming back from the fields at the end of the day. The boiling of her best clothes for the Harvest Festival. Mrs. Kowalski at the kitchen table: "Remember, Magda, men are like dogs—the more you scratch at their heads the more they turn to the one that kicks them."

Babula laughing.

The cool of the church high on the hill above Mokre. The wooden beams like the trees in the forest. The dancing in the evening. Dancing with the boys from Karlikov. Drunken Brunon Dudek singing his sad songs as the night turned to morning.

No, she had not gone back.

And now in the darkness. Ivan. Everything else gone.

There was something she wanted to ask. But she could not think of a way to put the words.

She heard his breathing deep and loud.

Babula told you, *Love will grow slowly, like an apple tree.*

Babula—folding the blankets.

But how will I know?

You will know, little one.

Babula opening the big wooden chest and placing the blankets inside. *Come. Have a look.*

The chest smelled of cedar, and clean linen.

My wedding chest, Babula says.

It had seemed so big and wide and deep then.

And this thing was not growing slowly like an apple tree.

• • •

Thundering heartbeats. His fingers on her face like tangled jolts.

She could smell him. His hair, his skin.

"Ivan—" she whispered.

The sound of his breath was all about her ears. In her hair. On her neck.

"Don't be afraid," he whispered in her ear.

And she did not tell him to stop when he kissed her then and held her close. In the darkness of that moment it was everything.

And she could not tell if she was falling. With hope, and a strange longing, with hope of the dreams that young women dream. And the baking road along the river—*where the sun caught your hair, and you felt it blow about your eyes like the touch of a hand*—

In the flickering light all that had been lost lay down. And everything to come was uncared of. And it was like that, with nothing said and not much understood, that old familiar notions fell away and were burnt up on the flaming hearth which is called

Love.

The girl looked up with big hungry eyes. She was certain now. The crow *must* be a prince.

"Climb onto my back," said Crow. "I will carry you across this dark forest to a Great Hall. It is far away. When you are there you shall sleep on a wide bed by a warm fire. But you must never cry out—whatever spirits may come for you in the night—for if you make one cry of fright, my misery will be doubled."

16

"Get up—"

Magda felt Ivan's hand on her shoulder.

She sat up. Her bare feet cold. The fire just a heap of smoldering embers. "What is it?"

"I don't know. I heard something."

He was standing. Motionless. Hand on the curtain.

"How would anyone know we're here?"

He pointed to the fire, the last twists of smoke wisping up the chimney.

"Maybe it's an animal," she said.

Ivan put a finger to his mouth.

And then she heard it.

The sound of boots, biting in the snow outside.

She sat so still, and so quiet, that she forgot to breathe.

The footsteps stopped.

Ivan bent down, bringing his ear closer to the door.

The definite sound of voices. Faint outside.

Behind the door there was a clank, a draft of cold air. Ivan dropped the edge of the curtain like a hot coal.

A grubby hand held the mail slot open.

A nose poked in.

"I know you're in there," a voice sang.

There was shuffling.

The flap fell shut.

Silence.

Ivan grabbed the axe. "Get upstairs," he hissed, shoving Magda toward the steps.

She felt with her hands against the walls. Her bare feet cold on the steps. Her heart racing. Eyes wide with fear.

There was a banging on the boarded window.

Thud thud thud against the door.

The smell of smoke.

Something pushed through the mail slot, and then laughter. Flames licked up around the curtain. Ivan stamped at the ground. Ripped the curtain down. Beat at it.

Then he was up the stairs. In three strides. Pulling her with him.

"We'll climb out of the window."

"They'll be waiting outside," she said.

"Just go."

He pushed her inside the bathroom. Broken glass cutting her bare feet.

"Ivan—"

She heard him out on the landing.

Boom!

The outsiders beat at the door with something heavy. There was a crack of splitting wood. Words unintelligible. Grunting with each battering of the timbers.

For a moment everything was silent.

Then wood, ripping from the hinges.

"Yalla, yalla! We know you're in here," sang the voice again.

There was muffled laughter.

"We told you not to come back," another voice shouted into the darkness. "Blettin' told you bluds! We're gonna get you."

"Chewy, Scott."

The striking of flint. *Krrrk.*

The leader held up a lighter.

He was tall and lean. Already a man. Flesh stretched taut across his hard cheeks. Dry-skinned and pimpled. A weak jaw. Thin lips and hard cysts on his eyelids. Dangling from his hand was a lump hammer. He was wearing dirty jogging trousers tucked into old army boots. His upper body shrouded in a torn gray and black ski jacket. On his head two black woolen hats were pulled tight over a hooded top.

Behind him were two boys, breathing in the cold air.

"This is the blettin' heath, man," he shouted. He grinned at his crew. "You feel me? Our blettin' heath! You wanna come pinch our business sans invite, blud?"

He beckoned his pack.

Ivan stood in the darkness at the top of the stairs.

He saw the light moving downstairs.

"We're gonna be havin' you!"

The light advanced.

Fell on the stair.

135

Ivan crashed into the bathroom and slammed the door shut. Fumbling in the pitch-black, he turned the lock.

Magda grabbed at him.

"The window," he said.

There were thuggish footfalls on the stairs.

"Quick!"

Hammer blows fell on the door.

He felt for the edge of the bath, climbed up on it. Grabbing Magda's shoulder he kicked against the shutter and it clattered open.

Something smashed through the flimsy door.

Magda screamed.

"They're getting out the window, man."

"Get round the back and cut 'em off!"

"There's a blettin' gwai in there too, blud. I heard her."

Ivan clambered onto the shed roof, pulling Magda out through the broken window.

The hammer smashed again, splitting the door. A hand reached in, searching for the lock.

"My foot. Ivan!"

Magda's foot had caught in the window frame.

Ivan pulled her, his feet slipping on the icy roof, and they fell in a tangled mess, grabbing at the ridged tiles for purchase.

The courtyard was only a few feet below them. Away over the other side of the shed were the white-topped roofs of the abandoned houses. A steep drop onto the road below.

The two youths came into the courtyard. One of them clambered onto the water butt with a lump of wood in his hand.

At the window the bloody leader appeared, shrouded in his hooded coat, clambering through the broken shutters.

His eyes locked on Magda. "No fucking invite, bitch."

Ivan let go of her hand. She saw him silhouetted against the sky, the axe above his head. She was losing her grip. Her bare feet dangling over the drop to the road.

The leader of the gang came across the tiles. Ivan thrashed out at him with the axe. Caught his outstretched hand.

"Aaagh!"

Magda screamed. Her fingers could hold on no longer and she felt herself slide.

And in the dimness she saw Ivan above her, grappling with the man. His body swayed as if it were in slow motion. His feet slid on the icy tiles. He lost his footing and fell.

Down, down. Away on the other side.

"Ivan!" she screamed.

She felt herself slipping down over the roof, frozen tiles and bricks scratching and grazing her arms. Her legs scrabbling at nothing. An awful moment as she fell to the bottom of the wall. Half buried in a drift.

Bare feet stinging in the snow.

"Ivan!"

"The gwai's on the other side of the wall!"

"Run, Mag—"

Thwack!

Ivan's voice cut short.

"Blettin' hold him! I'll get her."

Magda pulled herself up.

Far off at the end of the street she saw the dark shapes of the trees.

She turned. And saw him.

His face hidden in the shadows under his hood.

He held up his broken fingers. "You're gonna pay for this." She saw the whiteness of teeth clenched in his face. "This is our turf. You done a bad choice coming here."

The other two youths dragged Ivan out onto the road.

He raised his head.

One of them punched him in the guts.

Vomit choked out onto the snow.

"Take him back." The man pointed toward the building looming over the pond.

"You need help?" one of the others shouted.

"No. I'm gonna take care of her."

Magda scrabbled onto her knees, pushed herself up off the ground with her hands. And ran.

She could hear him—behind her. Swearing and wheezing and grunting. Her feet, blocks of ice, falling *slap slap slap* on the sharp, freezing snow. Her coat, baggy and heavy and jumping about her with every footfall. The sound of the boots and that angry mouth so close.

"Come here, you stupid gwai bitch."

Head thrown back, cold wind forcing tears from her eyes. Running. Stumbling.

And then, up ahead, she saw lights. Just pinpricks dancing among the cobweb of branches.

The road!

She forced her legs heavy as lead and burning with pain. On, on.

Above her, above London, the first glimmers of cold light stole over the skyline, an ashen Valkyrie creeping pale fingers down between the gray buildings and empty streets behind the wire. She came to the fence. Fell against it. It shook and sagged and ridges of snow fell down in a shower. And clinging there, so close, Magda wondered if this was what was left of her, this animal part, and how she would survive it and which bit would die if he got her at last. And whether she had the strength and what would she do with her feet bare in this snow if she got away and how she would forgive herself if she did not go back for Ivan.

She hauled herself up, legs dangling and kicking, sticking her numb toes into the holes of the chain-link fence.

The man jumped for her. She felt a hand around her ankle.

"You stupid cow."

She kicked down and felt the side of his face against her bare foot and gripped the wire for her life, kicking and pulling.

"Help!"

She screamed it through the fence.

"Help!"

She felt the man's hand slipping around her leg. She stamped down with all her might.

The fence swayed and the wire juddered and her fingers slipped away. She fell down to the snow, hard on her back.

The man laughed. He took a knife from his pocket and flicked it open. "We're gonna have a little tumble now. Best you keep chewysuwy and act sweet."

Crow. Wings clapping the air, heavy claws ready, hard beak cawing. Laughing.

Poking from the snow was a fallen branch. She scrambled back on her elbows and grabbed it. It felt firm in her hands.

"You wanna play rough?" The man still cawing. Pushing back his hood.

She rose up. It was a rage. Cowed and sweated and shoeless and trapped.

She swung the branch with all her might.

He wasn't expecting it.

The branch was short and hard. As solid and heavy and unbending as stone.

The thud of wood against skull.

Thok.

His face. Eyes blinking in disbelief.

Magda, taut for more fight.

The man shuddering like a ninepin.

He fell. Like a rotten tree on shallow soil. Toppled. Roots and all. Stiff and straight, his startled face flat onto the snow.

Magda dropped the branch. Struggled to her feet with every nerve beating and clattering.

The man did not move.

She saw where her bleeding feet had marked the snow. And then she knelt down and with frozen fingers she clawed at the laces of his boots, glancing fearfully over her shoulder. But no one came. And she pulled them onto her bare feet.

Still warm.

And then she took a breath. A good hard breath.

Looked down at the body. Picked up his fallen knife from the snow.

Better to suffer for what is right, Magda.

And she turned, and ran. Her small dark shape disappearing back under the trees.

Better to suffer for what is right, than to do what is wrong, Magda.

17

Magda hid under the frost-rimed bushes at the edge of the ice and studied the building.

Four storys high.

The entrance—a dark doorway shadowed under a concrete porch.

Nothing moving.

She shuffled forward. Soon they would wonder about their friend.

There was a noise. A Jeep rolled between the trees. The same one they had seen at the hole in the ice. It crunched to a halt by the side of the pond; deep treads in the tires filled with snow. The engine cut and the doors opened.

Two men got out. The doors smacked shut. The men looked about. One of them went around to the back and opened the tailgate, and a liver-colored dog on a chain jumped to the ground. The other man went over to some bushes and pissed against a tree.

"How much we take tonight, Artem?"

The man zipped his trousers and turned around. "Five grand, I reckon. This fat ginger guy, he do thirteen minutes."

The dog barked.

"Hesht!" The man yanked on the chain.

"Covered in lard like fuckin' turkey!"

They laughed. One of them spluttered a thick cough and lit a cigarette.

"Better give rats their money."

The two men made their way up the bank, pushing at branches, stumbling and swearing at the snow.

Magda watched them go into the building. Disappearing into the dark open doorway.

She moved forward and crouched down behind a snow-banked wall.

It was so close. She felt the knife in her hands. Opened the blade. She could hardly feel her fingers.

Now.

The entrance hall was pitch-black. Noises echoed down the bare concrete stairs.

Up above, a door clicked open. Footsteps shuffled on the landing above her.

She ducked beneath the dank and musty stairwell. Moldering cardboard boxes stacked up in a pile. The stolen boots dug into the backs of her thighs as she crouched down with her back hard against the wall. Heart beating like a drum.

Bam bam bam.

The footsteps slapped down the stairs.

"—to get the shit, man? Always me, you feel me?"

Right above her head.

"Chewy, Scott."

"Yeah, but it's proper blettin' cold out there."

"I said shut your chewy muzzle."

She waited.

She heard the door of the vehicle out by the pond slamming shut.

Footsteps came back into the hallway.

"—this big! And where's Yusuf?"

"Havin' a bit of fun out on the heath with that gwai bitch! Romeo and Joo-liet, man!"

They laughed.

But they didn't go back up the stairs. She heard the footsteps come around beside the stairwell and stop. Right in front of where she hid. She could see their legs. A door opened.

"Yusuf's gonna be having him bad when he gets back with that gwai. How much you reckon we'll get for her?"

"Come on, man! Laters. Artem's gonna be cheatin' us out our share if we don't get back up there pronto pronto."

The door shut.

The footsteps shuffled back up the stairs.

Voices fading behind the clunk of a latch.

Magda slipped out from under the stairwell and reached with cold reluctant fingers for the handle of the door.

It seemed that the opening of doors led to bad things. Her feet creaking on the rough boards of the abandoned cottages in Morochov. Always things disappearing. Mama. Babula. The truck.

The shooting of the pony. Stopko's stale room in Krakow with the damp socks steaming on the radiator. The metal doors of the container clanging shut and that gold-toothed grin.

She turned the handle slow and quiet. Expecting the worst.

"Ivan?" she whispered into the stale darkness. There was a tiny window high up in the wall of the room, dry leaves on a deep sill. She saw an old motorbike resting on its stand in the gloom.

"Ivan? It's me. Magda."

She saw him. Slumped in the corner. Hands and feet tied.

"Ivan—"

Slowly, he lifted up his head.

She was at his side. Knife in hand. Sawing at the ropes.

She helped him up, and he steadied himself. Rubbed at his mouth. His face was swollen: a thick eye, blood on his cheek.

"There's a car, Ivan. Under the trees."

He stumbled on his battered leg. Something clattered to the floor. He leaned against the wall.

They waited. But no one came.

And then they were out on the snow.

"It's at the front. By the pond."

"How many of them?" he croaked.

"Two men and a dog. Many boys. I don't know exactly."

She supported him, his weight heavy against her shoulder. Limping down the bank. Slipping and sliding on the snowy ground, pushing at branches. Onto the ice.

The light was growing brighter. Birds beginning to sing unseen in the bare branches of the trees. They bundled along at the margins. To the vehicle. Ivan pulled himself into the cab, and Magda slipped into the driver's side and pulled the door closed. She felt the cold vinyl of the seat beneath her. The keys hanging from the ignition jangled against her knee.

It was a very old car. She studied the controls on the dashboard. Dials for speed and fuel and temperature. A radio bolted under the shelf.

She peered down at the gear stick. *You have never driven a car before. Only Stopko's old tractor.* She took a deep breath. *In the great sea of everything, driving this car is just a tiny drop. Imagine you have done it a thousand times.*

Ivan turned his head toward her. Dim clouds of light smudged through the trees and hovered over his face. "Can you drive?" he said.

"Not really. A tractor last summer."

He groaned.

She turned the key. The still-warm engine started, needles danced into life on the dashboard. She pushed her foot down onto the pedal and thrust the gear rudely into first. It ground loudly. She forced it again, revved hard. Smoke poured from the exhaust.

"*Blyad!* They will come!" Ivan hauled himself upright, turned his swollen face to look up at the building.

She took her foot off the clutch and they lurched forward and stalled.

Hands shaking. She turned the key again. Revved the accelerator.

"Quick!" Ivan shouted.

"I'm doing it. I'm doing it!"

The men were spilling out of the building, alerted by the noise.

146

The gang in a ragtag group behind them. The dog on its chain, leaping and barking.

She released the clutch. They lurched forward, bouncing across the ground toward the frozen pond.

"Go over the ice—"

"It won't hold us—"

"Just go, Magda!"

The gang pushed through the brambles and slid out, shouting. Magda jerked the wheel, swerving to avoid the dinghy frozen in the shallows, and they were out on the ice with a terrible creaking under the wheels.

"Don't stop!"

She gripped the steering wheel hard and stamped down on the accelerator.

"That way!" Ivan pointed. "The fence is that way."

The dog leaped at the window. Its slobber spraying the glass.

"Go, Magda!"

She pulled at the gear stick. Into second gear. She saw hands reaching out and the angry faces as the gang scattered, stumbling back on the ice. The car hit the bank and skidded up through the undergrowth. Something crunched against the underside of the chassis. A grating noise—and the back end jumped in the air. But on they went, branches smacking on the roof and tree trunks looming.

"There!" Ivan shouted.

Through the trees she saw the fence and the road behind it.

They had cleared the undergrowth.

The Jeep churned across the open ground, back end leaping and sliding as it tried to find traction in the deep snow.

"Now!"

They smashed through the fence. The steering wheel twisted from Magda's hands, wheels bouncing over the broken planks and wire, across the pavement, down the curb, and onto the road.

But she regained the steering wheel, swung right onto the street—with brambles trailing from the rear axle, engine screaming in second, and tires thick with snow.

And then they were gone.

Lost in the warren of snow-mired roads that stretched like tentacles across the great cold waking city.

The girl, Mary, got up and looked out the window at the moon-path reflected on the sea below.

"I was thinking that maybe I should leave the rest of the story for tomorrow?" she said. "It's late."

Willo stirred up the embers of the fire and threw on a log. "But I want to know what happens—and anyway, you can't stop a Tell until the good bit comes out at the end."

"Good bit?"

"You got to have some good happen," Willo said. "Else the child ain't never gonna sleep."

Mary sat back in her chair. "Well, I'm a long way from the end so you better skewer that fish and put it in the fire, because you won't be getting anything else for supper."

The dog pricked up its ears at talk of supper. Like sensible dogs do. And Mary put the baby to her breast and continued—

18

An English bull terrier—of the brindled variety: thick shoulders, muscular legs, prominent nose—cocked its leg against the freezing iron railings and relieved itself.

"Buller!"

It sniffed at the scent it had left and looked up, wagging a stiff tail at the old lady calling from across the street.

She waved her stick again.

"Buller. Come on now!"

But the dog ran on ahead. He jumped up against the low fence surrounding a playground. Barked at a pigeon sitting cold and hungry on a rusting set of swings. The bird mustered enough energy and flitted to the safety of a tree.

The old lady ambled along with her walking stick, muttering to herself.

The dog jumped to the ground and continued along the fence, firm paw prints marking the snow. There was an island of bushes up ahead. A small wild area where it could snuffle about at will.

"Buller!" the old lady called impatiently, her back hurting. Age was a dose of medicine she could have lived without. She leaned on her stick and gazed at the broken slide and seatless swings in the playground.

To be bringing up children. Here?

She thought of her husband, Ant, lying on a stretcher in the corridor of the hospital. "Look out for yourself, Bobby—"

She saw it all around now. Everything broken down. Dirty and overcrowded. It wasn't just the frozen water pipes and constant power cuts, the overcrowding and lawless gangs and lack of jobs and hardly any food in the shops all winter. No, worse than all that was the constant cold. Cold everywhere you went, all day, all night, hardly a break in it. Summer, if you could call it that, wet and stormy, and the first snows in October this year.

Everyone floundering in drifting uncertainties. Just waiting. Not caring who got into power, or what new initiative they were planning, or the whys and wherefores of it. All they wanted to know was: When is it going to get a bit warmer?

"I tell you, we're on our way to being a Third World country." Ant, turning his head on the dingy hospital pillow.

She heard a beating and throbbing along the cold bricks and stone. The sound of them coming.

"Buller!" There was a new urgency in her voice. The dog bounded over.

The street was empty. Just an old Jeep with steamy windows parked beside a boarded-up shop.

The old lady hurried on. The noise growing louder. She hobbled up the steps to her front door and fumbled with the key. Looking down, she saw that the basement flat still had an old mattress stuffed in the window against the cold. And they had a baby down there.

The fading sign nailed onto the front door rattled as she forced it open.

NO POLES
NO ASIANS
NO DOGS

You're all right, love, it's the foreigners I ain't gonna trust with one. Lettin' them shit all over the house, the landlord had said. *But you gotta have a dog to protect yourself at your age.*

"Come on, Buller!"

The door slammed shut behind her. She made her way up the worn linoleum on the stairs with her hand on the cold white rail and the dog worrying at her feet.

In her flat, laying her stick in the corner, she pulled down the metal shutters. Sat breathless in an armchair. Her dead husband smiling from a photo frame on the bookshelf.

"They'll pass, Buller. It's all right. They'll pass."

The noise drew nearer.

Sticks beating. A unified chanting. The words growing intelligible as a crowd streamed through the side streets. Police sirens wailing far off.

A woman's voice screeching through a bullhorn.

"Step up! Death stalks the streets! Men, women, and children. Come out and join us! Help us build the Ark."

The crowd answering in unison.

"FOR ALL OUR TOMORROWS!"

. . .

Magda had driven in a rush of adrenaline. Fearful of any passing shadow, she had parked in the first quiet street and locked the doors. It had started to snow again, the bright morning thickening with clouds. She shivered in the cold—listening to Ivan's loud rasping breaths.

Later, when he woke, she said:

"We have to keep going."

He sat up and looked through the window. "How much fuel do we have?"

"Half. The gauge says half."

Ivan climbed over the seat and into the back of the Jeep.

"What are you doing?"

"Seeing what else is back here." He unscrewed the lid on one of the jerry cans. Smelled it. Undid the strap and shook the can. Climbed back into the front seat.

"What will we do now?"

"We must go to Liverpool," he said. "Deliver the passports to Gulbekhian."

"And then what?"

"Gulbekhian will get us back to Krakow."

A flag of anxiety slapped up under her ribs.

It fluttered again, and a sickly nausea welled up in her throat.

"What if we run out of fuel?" Magda said.

"We will find a way."

She swallowed. Felt a hotness behind her eyes.

"You don't have to come if you are afraid," he said. "You can keep the money we have left. It's yours anyway. You can do what you want. Find your own way back."

"Five hundred zloty? It's nothing."

Ivan stared out the window. "You can come or not come. That is your choice. If you want to turn back now, I'll find my own way."

"I'm not afraid. Even if I have nothing. But I don't call that a choice!"

Ivan laughed.

"What?" she demanded.

"You. Angry."

"I am angry because you don't care if I come with you or not."

"They're just words, Magda." And he smiled and put his arm over her shoulder and pulled her close.

She felt like that dog, sidling close to a foot that kicks.

A police car flashed across the junction ahead. And an old woman with a dog hobbled past, up the steps of a building, slamming the front door behind her.

"Ivan—look."

A chanting mass of people had surged from a side street at the end of the road. Magda could see faces turned upward, challenging the boarded windows of the surrounding houses. The rampant yelling of a woman with a bullhorn led the mob.

"Come out and join us!"

Voices answered in unison.

"FOR ALL OUR TOMORROWS!"

Magda started the engine in a panic, crunched the gears into reverse and backed out of the alley. As the wheels dropped over the curb, she hauled the heavy steering wheel around.

The crowd was drawing nearer.

"WHADDAWE WANT?"

"FOODNPOWER!"

"WHENDOWE WANNIT?"

"NOW!"

There was the wailing of sirens. From a turning up ahead, a police car nosed into view.

And three squat riot vans, grilled windows dark and ominous, lumbered around the corner and fanned out, barricading the street. Army Jeeps screeched behind them, doors opened and soldiers jumped onto the road with guns and riot shields.

The woman leading the crowd stopped. Masses surging in the street behind her.

"We're trapped," Magda said.

The woman raised her arm, screamed into the bullhorn with renewed vigor.

"The time is made for action! Here is the sign! Step up! Death stalks the streets!"

A voice crackled through a speaker from the riot vans.

"Disperse now! We have live ammunition. I repeat. Disperse now. Do not advance!"

Something flew through the air and smashed on the ground. Flames licked across the snow.

"Drive, Magda!" Ivan shouted.

Someone waved a banner, screaming at the massed rows of police.

"Keep calm!" yelled the woman with the bullhorn. "We are a peaceful protest." The mob engulfed her. "You cannot obstruct us. Join us! We are all disenchanted! WHAT DO WE WANT?"

"FOOD AND POWER!" roared the crowd.

Smoke filled the air, smoke and the pushing crowd surrounding the car. Angry faces staring in.

There now pushed forward a determined motley collection of *others*. Noticeable suddenly by their clothing—their hats pulled down low, hoods obscuring their faces. Wearing dark glasses, welding goggles, and scarves, and with homemade weapons in their hands.

A man banged on the hood, an excited face turning away with a grimace. The man leaned back like a javelin thrower and threw a brick. There was screaming. The crowd split every which way.

"Stop!" screeched the woman into her bullhorn. "We are a peac—"

But her voice was cut short, and an angry bellowing broke out from the advancing front line.

A shout went up. "Cover your eyes! They've got SMUs!"

An incredible light pulsed from the riot vans. Hands went up to eyes, people turning, blinded by lasers that punched deep shadows among the crowd.

The determined group, prepared, surged forward in their goggles and glasses. A swelling throaty rage rose up. Interspersed with screaming—and the bellowing once more from the soldiers at the end of the street.

"YOU HAVE FIVE SECONDS TO DISPERSE!"

And then they opened fire.

The first volley of shots seemed to strike at random. There was an audible gasp. Bodies fell.

A rattling of shutters. Breaking of glass.

And then again.

A bullet ricocheted against a wall and pinged on the side of the Jeep. Stressed shards of masonry sprayed against the windshield.

Magda released the clutch—her hands like talons on the steering wheel. She would remember the faces, hazy in her blurred vision as she dodged the people, flashing like trees past a train window, leaping out of her way, two men dragging a body to the side of the road, people helpless, stumbling in their blinded panic.

She swung the wheel and swerved from a woman with blood on her face. She saw a narrow side road, people fleeing down it, blood and glass and bricks on the snow. The soldiers raised their guns again. Shouted through the speakers.

"Don't stop," Ivan shouted.

Magda fixed her eyes on the road ahead. Gear-clutch-accelerate, dog-legging crazily through the snowy streets, the sound of the roaring engine rising above the yells and shouts. She was aware of the snowflakes spitting angrily on the windshield and the mob of running people disappearing from the mirror. Vaguely she felt that her feet were cold on the juddering pedals of the old Jeep, and smelled the smoke in the air.

And they were away.

19

A short wiry man with tatty hair the color of straw heard the whistling dip and rise of the police siren and slunk quickly down an alleyway that led behind an abandoned warehouse. Above two metal doors at the back of the building the words COOL TOWN SQUAT were painted in fading letters on the dirty gray bricks.

The man's name was Rory Moss.

Rory pulled a key from his pocket and rattled it in the low keyhole, pulling the rolling doors up and over and closing them with a clang behind him.

He peered into the cavernous workshop, eyes adjusting to the dingy light. He slung the rucksack off his back, took out a roll of tools, and threw a siphon hose and a crowbar down on the oily workbench where he had been breaking an engine for parts that morning. In one corner the chimney from a large unlit woodburner disappeared through a crude hole in the brickwork.

He fumbled in the semidarkness and lit a paraffin lamp, then filled the tank of a generator with the last of the diesel from a jerry can. He pulled the starter cord—the generator thumped into life, and he connected jump leads to a bank of tractor batteries on the floor. Digging around in the pocket of his coat, he pulled out a battered mobile phone, which he plugged into a trailing extension cable.

Turning down the lamp, he tramped up a dusty stairwell at one end of the workshop, with his thin-soled boots scuffing on the dirty concrete steps.

At the top of the landing, he bashed on a door.

"Tom! Open the feckin' door," he shouted in a faded Irish lilt.

There was a short wait.

"That you, Rory?" came a muffled voice.

"Who the feck do you think it is?"

The door opened and a scruffy-looking man stood in the light. "You find any more diesel?"

"Did you?" Rory pushed past him into a wide corridor, boots clumping on the bare boards.

The scruffy-looking man shot the bolts with a scowl and followed Rory into the kitchen. "I was just asking..."

Rory took off his hat and laid it on the table. A girl sat there smoking a thin tarry roll-up and she looked over and smiled a dirty-toothed smile.

Someone was asleep under a blanket on an old sofa pushed against the wall.

Rory put his rucksack down on the floor. The girl got up, brushed strands of long mousy hair off her face. "You get any food?"

"Yes. In the bag."

"Shall I make some tea then?" she said, pulling the long fraying ends of her sweater down over her hands.

Rory looked at her. Grubby face, greasy hair, clothes that needed washing, dirty boots like his; the floor was filthy, the bare boards dark and grimy, and the snow had started to fall again behind the window, from the tiny rectangle of gray sky visible between the grim-faced backs of the warehouses. "Jayzus."

"Where are the others?" he said.

"Asleep," said Mousy Girl, placing a large kettle on the range.

"Well, they could get their lazy feckin' arses out of bed and help tidy this shitehole up a bit." He delved into his rucksack and pulled out a stash of food: bread, two eggs, a bag of salt, a sealed plastic bag of milk and a pile of withered parsnips and green potatoes, and a large limp cabbage. He left the two bottles of cheap vodka in the bag.

"Put the radio on," he said.

Mousy Girl plugged in a small radio and fiddled with the dials.

Krrchk "—in London last night. And now over to Shana on the M40. Shana—"

They sat silently, listening.

"—we'd seen the worst chaos yesterday, but both lanes are still solid with traffic. The jams must go on for forty miles in each direction."

"And what are the weather conditions like right now, Shana?"

"Pretty bad. More power lines came down last night. Large stretches of the motorway remain unplowed."

"And do we have any idea where all these people are going?"

"I spoke to one couple"—rustling of paper—"on the northbound carriageway. They'd come from Oxfordshire. They said they'd been cut off for most of January. But, John, a lot of the vehicles on the motorway have been abandoned. Which is causing more problems for the snowplows when they arrive."

Sound of distant bullhorn: *"Get back in your cars. Get back in your cars."*

"We didn't catch that, Shana—"

"People from the countryside report being cut off all winter without power."

"And do we know where they're going?"

"No. There's no order to it. We've heard of makeshift camps on the outskirts of major cities. There has been talk of enforced billeting if the situation continues."

"And presumably many of the travelers are heading south. To London."

"Yes. That's right."

"And do we know how many people are leaving?"

"No. It's impossible to tell. It's chaos out here. It's not just people leaving the countryside, but others leaving the cities due to the rioting."

"Do the police and army appear to have the situation under control yet?"

"I'm here with Captain Morley of the Royal Scots Fusiliers. He's been overseeing the exodus here in Oxfordshire. Captain Morley—do you think your forces have got the situation under control?"

"Good evening. Yes. Obviously with such unprecedented numbers moving toward the larger towns and cities there have been problems. And of course there are stragglers left behind. But we're advising people to stay put, to wait for—"

A shot. Shana's voice: "Oh my God!" Another shot. Sound of

microphone rustling. Long pause. "Sorry. John? Yes. There has been a disturbance on the road just beneath us."

A man's angry voice over a bullhorn: *"Get back in your vehicles! Get back!"*

"Shana. Are you all right?"

"Yes. Yes. But—I've never seen anything like it." Microphone rustling. "The situation here is terrible—"

"Shana? Shana? . . . Well, I'm sorry about that. We seem to have lost contact with our reporter on the M40. We'll get back to her as soon as we can.

"Other breaking news: with the deepening energy crisis, Runya Karr, Governor of Germany, admitted today that the Central European government was closing Germany's borders to travel, along with France, Poland, Hungary, Austria and—"

There was a muffled sound—off microphone—whispers.

"—I'm going to have to interrupt this with"—rustling—"a broadcast. From the prime minister."

There was a clicking and buzzing.

"This is your prime minister speaki—. . . inform you that the government, under the auspices of the Civil Contingencies Act . . . a State of Emergency to be reinstated across the United Kingdom with immediate effect."

"Bloody hell!" said Mousy Girl.

"Shhh!"

"—at eighteen thirty Greenwich Mean Time. I repeat: a State of Emergency has been declared. The police and army are armed."

The radio message repeated itself and Rory switched it off.

A snowball splatted on the windowpanes.

A muffled shout from the yard outside.

"Let me in, man!"

Rory pushed back his chair, went to the window, and looked down.

"It's me. Biggy. Let me in!"

Rory opened the window, a wedge of snow falling into the yard below. A blast of cold air welled into the room.

"What the feck, Biggy?" he shouted down.

"Just let me in, man. I'm telling you. Let me in. They're coming."

"Who?"

"Blettin' medevils, man. And soldiers with guns."

Rory shut the window, slouched down the stairs to the workshop, and hauled up the garage doors. Biggy darted inside, snow on his shoulders.

"Shut the blettin' doors, blud. It's the chungdys from the Woodberry Down Estate. Fighting, man. Started out on Seven Sisters. Medevil bluds doing their nut with the dogboyz. Feckin' soldiers with guns, man. Real feckin' guns! It's mental out there."

"How did it start?"

"Dunno. Just came round the corner and there's all these bluds in their long shirts doing their nut with the Woodberry posse."

"Haven't you heard the news?"

"What news, man?"

"State of Emergency. Get away from the doors." Rory connected two heavy-duty jump leads to the terminals on the tractor batteries, followed the wires to a pair of bare clamps, and attached them to the metal doors of the workshop. They sparked as he made contact. "No feckin' marginul's going to get in here."

Far off, the sound of trouble began to rumble up through the cold bricks and along the dirty, snow-covered streets.

He could hear it now.

Back upstairs the others were huddled around the window.

"Blow out the light, man, blow out the light," Biggy whined.

The noise grew louder.

"Look!"

An orange glow. Black smoke. Buildings on fire just streets away.

Downstairs, the metal shutters on the street-side windows clanged. Sticks trailed along the walls. *Tak tak tak tak tak tak.*

The peaking, dipping roar of an angry crowd could be heard now.

A vehicle screeched down the road.

"Look!" Mousy Girl pointed out across the roofs.

A huge mushrooming cloud of black smoke billowed up from the houses behind the warehouse; an orange glow licked over the tiles.

They could smell it now.

There was an explosion that shook the windows.

"We've got to get out."

"What?"

Rory pulled on his coat, took his bag from the floor. "It's on fire! We'll be next. Get out of here."

As if to prove his point the flames roared out in spiraling

fingers across the yard. Sucking the oxygen with a rushing wind. The air so thick with smoke you could hardly see the next roof.

"You do what you shiting well like. I'm out of here . . ."

• • •

Magda and Ivan were lost in the warren of streets. The engine spluttered. Magda pumped at the accelerator. There was a car coming up fast behind them. Growing closer on the icy road. She changed gear and the exhaust putted ominously. The car behind sounded its horn.

Ivan looked back over the seat. "You need to move over."

She panicked, ran the vehicle up onto a bank of snow. Their engine died and the passing car—piled high with blankets and boxes and children crammed in seats—reeled by, horn blasting.

She looked in the mirror. A man was walking fast along the side of the road. He had seen them stop and, pulling a rucksack close over his shoulder, he was soon upon them.

"What shall we do?" Magda hissed.

The man rapped on the window. "Hey. Can you give me a lift?"

"What do I tell him, Ivan? He wants a lift."

"Ask him if he knows the way to Liverpool."

Magda wound the window down a bit. "We go north," she said. "To Liverpool. But we have problem with the car."

• • •

"—that's why they're so great. These old Niva Jeeps. Pretty much mend them with a crowbar and a spanner." Rory Moss rummaged in his rucksack and looked nervously over his shoulder. Pushed a strand of dirty blond hair behind his ear. "But there's trouble on the streets tonight, my friends. So we'd better be quick."

The hood was propped open. He leaned over the wing, his long fingers blackened with oil, reaching around in the engine. Occasionally he cupped his hands to his mouth and blew into them.

"So you were just driving along and the power died?"

Magda nodded.

"Have you got fuel?"

"About a quarter full, I think."

"You probably stirred up a load of shite in the fuel line and the filter's blocked."

He followed the fuel pipe back up from the carburetor and found the filter.

"What does he say?" asked Ivan.

"I'm not sure, something with the fuel."

"Can he fix it?"

The man turned. "What's that?"

"He ask if you can fix it," Magda said.

"Yeah," Rory grunted, turning a spanner on the nut. "Come on, you little—aagh!" The nut released and he undid the bolt. "So what are your names then?"

"I am Magda."

Diesel ran out of the fuel pipe and he held it up. "I'm Rory. Here, hold your finger over this."

Magda pushed in beside him and held the pipe.

"And your friend?" Rory said.

"He is called Ivan."

But Ivan stood apart, distrustful and silent.

Rory cast a glance at him with narrow eyes and took the filter to pieces in his frozen fingers. *These kids are definitely illegals.* "Yup. Blocked. Look." He held out the little piece of wire mesh. It was thick with sludgy detritus. He tossed it down in the snow. "Don't need it anyway." He pushed the casing back together, fitted the filter back onto the fuel line, and tightened the nuts. "You got more fuel?"

"In the back," Magda said.

Rory fetched one of the jerry cans and sloshed it about. "You must have three hundred quids' worth of diesel here, kiddos." He filled the tank, fuel cap wedged between his knees. "Let's see if she'll start."

Ivan nudged her, whispered.

Rory didn't understand the words, but he understood the look.

"Don't worry—I'm not going to nick it, you can tell him." He got in, jiggled the gear stick, looked in the mirror out of habit, and turned the key in the ignition. The fuel pump ticked—*trrrrrrrr, trrrrrrrr*—and the engine started. He floored the accelerator. Smoke mushroomed from the exhaust.

"So you want to get to Liverpool then?" he said, stuffing his rucksack into the footwell. "Sounds good to me—"

20

"Shite!"

Magda jolted awake.

The Jeep slid on the ice, snow creaking in the tread of the tires. They came to a stop, skewed across the road. Rory Moss banged on the steering wheel again. "Shite!"

Snow had blown from the open fields. Wind-cut snow dunes sparkling in the headlights. The drifts were a meter high, blocking the single lane of the empty motorway.

"We'll have to wait until the morning. The plows won't be out again until then. If we're lucky."

They climbed out from the cab, doors clanging shut in the hollow cold, fumes steaming from the exhaust. Rory kicked at the frozen ridges. "Better dig ourselves a lay-by and hole up." He looked out at the darkening wasteland. "Should have turned in earlier—somewhere with some trees at least."

"What did he say?" Ivan asked.

Magda tucked her chin into her collar and looked about the desolate fields. "He says we'll have to wait until the morning. We will have to be patient, I think."

In the back of the Jeep, she pulled the blankets over her head. Wishing that Ivan would come back and crawl under them too.

But he did not.

. . .

She woke from a fragile, uncomfortable sleep. It was just morning. The sky was a slit of red on the horizon.

In the front, Rory coughed, took a swig from a bottle of vodka, and rolled himself a cigarette. "Here she comes."

"What?" said Magda, climbing into the front beside Ivan.

"The plow."

Steaming up the road, an army plow cut through the drifts, banking clouds of dirty snow onto the central barrier.

The plow passed. Huge wheels churning and flailing snow. It was followed by an endless line of army trucks with snow-clearing equipment chained up on massive trailers. The convoy rolled its way westward. Unstoppable and orderly.

Rory started the engine then wound down the window and threw his cigarette butt out in the ruts. "Right. We'll follow them. At a distance."

. . .

They had to drive slowly. The sky was low and gray, but it did not snow. The day wore on. The convoy had disappeared from view. They refueled with the last of the diesel.

FUEL AVAILABLE 2 MILES, FRANKLEY

Rory peered at the flapping homemade sign. "We're a good way past Bristol. Strange we haven't seen any traffic." He leaned down and tried the radio again. "Still nothing. Never mind, I'll ask at the garage. Hope they've got fuel."

But the plow had heaped a great wall of dirty crumbling snow barring the slip road. They could see the low, white roofs of the service station down in the dip. Metal slatted shutters pulled down at the windows. A few abandoned vehicles buried under drifts in the empty car park. And nothing moving.

• • •

The outskirts of a city appeared, snow-topped roofs of small settlements emerging from the fields at the side of the motorway.

"Is this Liverpool?" Magda asked.

"No. Birmingham."

"Is Liverpool far?"

"Depends on what you mean by fa—Jayzus, what now?" Up ahead three army Jeeps and cones across the lane. Several cars had come to a stop and soldiers moved along the line, talking through windows and waving the vehicles up to a slip road on the left.

"Right, you two. Don't say anything." Rory slowed to a stop and wound down the window. "What's the problem, Officer?"

There was the crackling of a walkie-talkie.

"Where are you going?"

"Liverpool."

"The road's blocked."

"So what am I meant to do?"

"There's an emergency shelter at Shrewsbury Hospital—you'll have to go there. Army plows are keeping the road clear until dark."

"Can I go back into Birmingham?" said Rory.

"No. There's a curfew."

"And the motorway? When can I get back on my way?"

"I can't say. You have to move on now, sir."

Rory wound the window up and followed the other cars being waved on to the Springfield slip road. With the flashing orange lights of the patrol vehicles blinking against the windshield. They were silent. Tense in their seats until they had pulled onto the Shrewsbury bypass with the roadblock behind them.

"That was a feckin' stroke of luck," Rory breathed out. "Cos I bet you twos don't have any papers for this car, do you?"

• • •

Progress was torturous. Clouds had been banking in the sky all day and now the first snowflakes began to spot the windshield and the tops of the roadside trees were gushing wildly in a growing wind.

Soon the snow was pelting down thick and relentless. The windshield wipers thrashed ineffectually. And, past Telford, conditions grew considerably worse. It was hard not to watch the dancing fuel gauge. Rory swigged at his bottle of vodka and dark thoughts crossed his mind.

The outskirts of Shrewsbury appeared. Up ahead in a stand of trees was a lay-by. He slowed down and pulled over into it. The wind howled about the car, battering it in shaking blasts. He turned the engine off. Flashing snowflakes faded in the darkness as the headlights died.

"Why are you stopping?" said Magda.

"See those lights up ahead?"

She peered into the blur of the falling snow. A flashing orange light pulsed above the bushes on the embankment.

"It'll be a roadblock. They're going to want to see your identity cards, maybe papers for the car."

"Are you sure?"

"Yes."

"So what will we do?"

"I'm thinking."

"Can we turn back?"

"Doubt it."

They got out. A coarse wind cut across from the north like a blade. It slammed the car door against the bodywork.

Rory sank to his waist in a snow-filled drainage ditch on the other side of the verge, waded up out of it, and gestured for them to follow.

They climbed up the embankment.

"Over there. Look."

They followed the direction of his arm.

An electricity pylon was visible in the dusk: angular metal struts rising above a copse of woodland in the distance.

"In the wood there," Rory said, "we can collect some firewood. There's a storm coming in tonight, but maybe there will be fuel deliveries by Monday, if we can sit tight till then. You two go and get some wood and I'll scout along further up and get a better look at the roadblock."

"But—"

"Come on. Or we'll freeze our feckin' arses standing here

talking. I'll meet you back here." He trudged away from them along the top of the embankment, turning once to wave, his figure growing small and dim in the snowstorm.

"Where is the key for the car?" Ivan shouted above the wind.

"He has it, I think," Magda said uneasily.

Ivan looked out across the field to the woodland. There was the shadow of a low building beside the copse of trees.

"I don't like it, Magda."

"Well, we better get some wood. Like he said. We'll freeze standing here."

• • •

Rory ducked into the scrubby bushes on the embankment and crouched down. God, it was cold! He took the near-empty bottle of vodka from his pocket and knocked back the dregs, then threw the bottle down onto the snow. He could see the two kids halfway across the field. He kept an eye on them until they had disappeared into the copse of trees, then he leapt down the bank, jogged breathlessly along the road, and slipped into the lay-by.

His heart pounded as he yanked open the door of the Jeep and slid onto the cold seat. He took the key from his pocket and started the engine. And with a hesitant glance up the bank he eased the vehicle out onto the icy road. The wheels gained traction on the packed snow. And Rory Moss, unencumbered at last, headed toward Shrewsbury, past the flashing orange light—not of a roadblock, but the army snowplow—with a good vehicle and the promise of food and shelter obliterating any vestiges of decency that may have lingered in his vodka-addled mind.

21

The clanking caterpillar tracks of a British Army PistenBully utility vehicle mashed their way over the deep snow under the electricity pylons. Traversing the rough terrain and sizable drifts with ease.

It was seven o'clock in the morning and a low, slanting light caught the side of the cab, illuminating the crisp white letters painted on the standard green British Army livery: ΛΝΡΕC.

The Asian energy giant that sponsored the MOD's patrol infrastructure capabilities.

Inside the cab were two soldiers on line-inspection duty. It was an easy day's work. No standing around in the wind marshaling traffic, or digging snowdrifts back at base, or enduring the hellish boredom of a tactical deployment meeting in some overheated prefab office in Birmingham.

They simply powered along under the Wylfa pylons, checking for faults and wires down. Hot air blasted from the under-dash fans and loud music pumped from the speakers.

"Are we going to refuel, Sarge?" Private Connors shouted above the pounding bass line.

"Yeah, next depot."

Connors gave a thumbs-up, his head nodding in time to the music.

They had circumnavigated Shrewsbury and ahead of them the cross braces of the next pylon rose in the sky, power lines swaying in the gale. They churned past it, snow flailing from the track plates.

"It's not far," Sergeant North shouted. "We can get a brew on."

The Shrewsbury Service Depot came into view. A long corrugated shed at the side of the track. The Bully slowed, crunching to a halt.

They jumped energetically from the cab, standard-issue Snotex boots sinking in the powder of last night's fresh fall. The thump of music deadened as they slammed the doors shut.

"Sarge! It's unlocked." Connors pushed the door to the depot shed open.

"What?"

"When was the last stop here?"

"Monday."

They peered into the dark. Connors pulled down the light switch—a generator automatically rumbled to life and a fluorescent strip light pinged and flashed.

Sergeant North paced along the line of snow-clearing vehicles and hydraulic platform trailers.

"Everything looks in order. You fill up the ancillary tanks, Connors, and I'll go and see what MCRs we've got in barracks. I'll make a report in the log about the breach." He unlocked a door in the corrugated paneling and went into the emergency barracks room built into the end of the shed. No windows, but bunks, the back-up generator, and hopefully a good supply of tea, coffee, and ration pouches.

In the depot, Connors, humming to himself, scuffed his way across the concrete floor between the fuel trailer and a spanking new Wassau Snowblower. The fuel hose was coiled at the rear of the tank and he began to haul it off the reel.

"What the f—" He dropped the hose. "Sarge!"

He nudged the toe of his boot against the huddled figures. "Oy! Get up!"

A boy. A girl.

He pulled the gun from his belt.

"Sarge! Get in here quick!"

Sergeant North stuck his head out the door. "What?"

"We've got company."

Magda saw two clean-shaven faces staring down at her.

"What the hell are you doing in here? This is government property."

"We—we have no place to sleep—"

"Oh, Christ. Foreigners. Right. Show us your identity cards." Connors hauled Magda up by the shoulder.

She looked at the soldiers. From one to the other.

"Identity cards!"

"What is it?" said Magda.

"You no speaky English?"

"Come on," said the sergeant. "They're just kids." He pulled his colleague's hand away from Magda's shoulder. "You got identity cards, love? Passport?"

Magda stared, helpless. "No. We have no passport."

"Bloody perfect," said Connors. "Now we'll have to take them back to base. It'll eff up our time sheet."

"What. You. Do. Here?" said Sergeant North. Speaking slowly to make himself understood.

"It is very cold in night—we were looking for place to sleep."

"Yeah, and I'm looking for bloody Jesus Christ," said Connors. "But he ain't here, is he?"

Sergeant North spoke again. "Look, I'm sorry, love, but without an identity card or passport I'm going to have to take you and your friend back to base. I have the right to arrest you for trespassing on government property. Do you understand?"

She nodded.

Ivan, who had been standing silent, leaned close. "They will find the passports if they search me. What are they saying?"

"They are arresting us for having no identity papers."

"What did your friend say?" snapped Connors.

"He just ask what will happen now," said Magda, heart pounding.

"Where are you from?"

"Poland."

"What are you doing out here?"

"We give lift," said Magda. "We give lift to man but he leave us on road and drive away. He take our papers in car. My mother live in London. Look, I have address here." She fumbled in her pocket and pulled out the scrap of paper. "Here. It is in London. We can go back to the road. Please let us go."

Sergeant North looked at the piece of paper.

"It's just cock and bull, Sarge. They're illegals. Look at them."

"Give them a break. You hungry, love?"

Magda nodded.

"I'll make them a brew. You fill the tanks."

"I wouldn't trust them more than a tart in barracks."

"I'll worry about that, Connors. They're just kids—lucky they haven't frozen to death." He turned to Magda. "You tell your friend, love. I'll get you something to eat."

In the barracks room, Sergeant North made some tea and gave them both a soup ration. He switched on a space heater.

"Sit down there." He motioned to two chairs and they sat, gulping down the hot food.

"So," he began, pulling a logbook from the shelf above the table, "what are two Polish kids doing out here? I assume you're aware that there's a State of Emergency across Britain at the moment?"

"My mother lives in London. She has a job there. I show you the address . . ."

Sergeant North sighed. "Yes. You showed me. But if your mother is in London, what are you doing in the middle of nowhere in this weather?"

"We drive to Liverpool and we give the man a lift. But then he steal the car."

"Yes, but why were you going to Liverpool in the first place?"

"I—We try to visit—We try to visit my uncle. He is ill."

"So you and . . ."

"He is my brother."

179

"So you and your brother left London, where your mother works, to visit your uncle in Liverpool? In a State of Emergncy with a storm coming down?"

"Yes."

"Have you got an address for this uncle, a number?"

Magda shook her head.

"And where did you get a car from?"

"It was—my mother's."

"Right. Your mother's car. Must be a good job she's found herself. Well, she's not going to be too pleased it's been stolen, is she?"

"Yes. No . . ."

It was Sergeant North's turn to shake his head. "And your passports were in the car."

"Yes. The man take them too. That is why we are here."

"I've got to be honest, love, but *that* is the biggest cock-and-bull story I've heard in a long while."

"Cock and bull?"

"Never mind."

"What will you do with us?"

"You'll have to come back to base and the police will take it from there." He tried a smile. "If they find your details, you can be on your way to visit this sick uncle or whatever."

Magda said nothing. Ivan nudged her questioningly.

Sergeant North finished his report in the logbook, snapped it shut, and got up. "Right. Wait here." He went out of the room, and appearing to have second thoughts, locked the door behind him.

. . .

Outside, Connors was filling the tanks, the heavy rubber hose from the fuel tank snaking across the snow. He looked up. "What are we going to do with them then, Sarge?"

"Well, they've got no identity cards so we'll have to take them back with us."

"It's a pack of lies. Someone probably gave them a lift and kicked them out at a roadblock." He withdrew the hose, dripping diesel onto the snow. "Maybe we should just let them go. They haven't nicked anything. Who'd know? They're not going to tell anyone."

"What, let them out? Here?"

"Why not. Save us a lot of bother."

"Look, Connors, you dump a wild fox into unknown territory and before you know it it's pilfering the bins and you've got to get someone to come out and deal with it. No, we just lock them in the back of the transport, carry on with the recce, and swap them over to the Dolgellau team coming back this afternoon. They can take them back to base."

"Don't we need clearance for that kind of thing?"

"Unless they've got oxyacetylene torches stuffed up their jumpers, they aren't going to get out of the transport in a hurry."

"Whatever you say, Sarge."

Sergeant North went back to the barracks room and unlocked the door. "Right, you two. Come with me. And don't try anything funny."

They followed him outside.

"We'll transfer you to another team heading back to base." He opened the heavy double-skinned steel door of the carrier.

Ivan looked about at the snow-whipped wilderness, at the gun in the soldier's belt.

"Come on. In you get."

They climbed up through the low door. The small cab had double-glazed windows on all sides and two padded benches big enough to seat four men. It was warm inside; hot air blew from a vent under the seats. The soldier slammed the door shut, locked it, and then climbed into the cab at the front of the vehicle.

"What time is it, Sarge?"

"It's eight. We should get to Dolgellau by thirteen hundred."

"You reckon those two are going to be all right stuck in there all day?"

"We'll let them out at the halfway depot for a piss and a brew. They'll be fine. They survived last night in the shed."

Connors glanced through the rear windshield.

"They're busy talking to each other back there."

"Well, they've probably got a lot to talk about."

"What'll happen to them?"

"They'll end up at Ravenscar detention center until spring if they're illegals. And then the first bus back home."

"To Poland?"

"Wherever they come from."

"Must be pretty bad over there if they think it'll be better in Liverpool."

Sergeant North laughed. "Well, it's not our problem,

Connors. You just keep your eyes on the line. That's what we're doing—remember."

Connors turned up the music. "Let's see if we can do it in four and a half, Sarge."

. . .

But Sergeant North—having never traveled in the personnel cab in the back of the Bully—had made an error in his reckoning. The vehicle he was driving at speed through the pristine new-fallen snow was designed for transporting personnel working in extreme weather conditions. Dangerous conditions.

Kitted out with all safety features.

And in the carrier, several feet behind him, under the back window, just beside Magda's knee, was a small, red, glass-fronted box. Emblazoned across it were the words:

LIFE AXE
EMERGENCY ESCAPE HAMMER
STRIKE SHARPLY ON GLASS

22

The Bully crunched to a halt in a large plantation of Norway spruce. Connors looked back into the carrier. The girl was staring at him. He looked away.

"Here." Sergeant North thrust a high-vis jacket at him, and they bumped shoulders in the small cab, the bulky garments rustling as they pulled them on, taping down the Velcro cuffs.

Connors pocketed the field binoculars and a waterproof notebook. "I hate this effing bit of the line."

Sergeant North opened the door. A prickly coldness filled the warm cab. "Jesus, it's cold." He looked up at Magda and Ivan in the carrier. Held up his fingers. "Ten minutes," he shouted through the glass.

"Feel a bit sorry for them," Connors said as they tramped through the thick snow between the trees.

"They'll be all right. Safer with us than out wandering in the snow like a couple of lost dogs."

. . .

"Can you see them?" Ivan said.

"No. They are away under the trees."

"Take off your coat. Quick."

She pulled it off her shoulders.

"We will have to be fast."

"Then what?"

"Run."

"But they will see our footsteps."

"We will run back along the tracks and then into the trees." He took out the hammer. It was small but heavy, a sharp point at one end. He cracked it sharply against the windowpane. The point cracked a hole.

"Harder, Ivan. Quick." She glanced back into the forest.

Ivan struck it harder. The glass made a strange creaking sound and cracks radiated from the hole. A shard fell out.

"Give me your coat!" He stuffed it against the glass and wedged himself against the seat. He lifted one leg and kicked as hard as he could. Cold air rushed into the cab. He kicked again and more chunks of glass fell out, a jagged hole in the window.

He clambered out feetfirst.

Magda followed. He helped her slide through the opening, ripped the coat out of the window, and then they set off, running back behind the vehicle in the rutted tracks, breathless and throwing glances over their shoulders.

"Now!" Ivan jumped over the banks of snow into the dark of the conifer plantation. Magda followed, adrenaline pumping, sweat rising, the snow flailing up around her legs.

And as he ran, ahead of her, Ivan was laughing.

Laughing and laughing. He turned. "We made it!"

• • •

They reached the edge of the plantation. It was bitter out in the open, and the cold rapped as unrelenting as a stone—icy in the blood that welled like treacle in their fingers and toes. There was a nonsmell to that kind of cold. The earth purged of scent, anaesthetized. It dried up your nostrils with every frosted breath. Sat in the hollows and beat from the ground.

In the afternoon light, with the sun setting behind the hills, they could see a wide valley rolling away before them, with brushy stands of bare hedgerows poking up frosted fingers from the ditches and culverts that marked the boundaries of buried meadows and obliterated roads. A great unknown landscape in which they were cast, alone, their human smallness weighing upon them as they surveyed the emptiness. From the other side of the valley, the silhouetted bulk of a mound-shaped hill rose up against the graying sky. The last light charging the snow with purpling shadows. Intermittent flashes of light blinked to the east.

"What are the lights?" said Magda.

"I don't know."

"Do you think there are people out here?"

"Perhaps."

"Maybe we should go back?"

"We were in that vehicle all day, Magda. For hours."

Magda glanced at the side of his face, the firm set of his mouth. "Well, what then?"

"We will cross the valley. There will be somewhere to hide, make a camp and a fire. Maybe people and food."

She followed his gaze and shivered. The snowflakes started to fall again. Not wet and soft, but dry and hard. Enough of a powder to cover their footprints if it kept up.

Overhead came a droning sound. Two large cargo planes. They ducked under the cover of the trees and watched them pass.

"Do you think they are looking for us?" she said.

Ivan pulled his collar up. "Us? No. You maybe." And he grinned at her.

• • •

Love was not slow and steady like a growing apple tree. It was not like Babula had said. There were many things Babula had said. Were all of them just fairy tales you tell to children?

Because Magda felt drawn to every fiber of Ivan's being. His angular jaw and the turning down at the corners of his lips and the flash of skin at his neck and the broad feel of his strong back and even right down to the tips of his toes.

All these new things that she had never imagined before.

No—this feeling was not slow, but savage like a stone smashing glass.

Ivan was right. She could have turned back a long time ago. But a seed had rooted inside her. And now she felt that she would follow him to the ends of the earth if he let her.

• • •

And what of Ivan?

He had been forged in the happenings of childhood, poured and cast into a certain mold. Like a bird that had been reared by human hand, he had imprinted upon his eye the vision of one face only.

The thin, sharp face of Anna. The girl in the Kiev orphanage who had held his hand and told him to forget. It was she who had reached out as the dark waters dragged Ivan away from shore. She had hauled him up into a leaking boat and they had tossed and pitched on the choppy waters of their childhood, together.

It was not Ivan's failing to be stuck on that vision. Because men are like dogs in many ways. They are not fickle. And that imprint would remain. That human face.

There was a weight to Magda; he had felt it. That feeling of something solid and right, clunking to earth and resting beside him.

But Ivan was not perhaps very brittle, despite his flaws. And unless he were to fall—to be shattered and break open—his softness would remain hidden: those cracks that can hide inside the hardest stone.

All Ivan knew was that no one had seen his tears. No one had seen them except the girl from the children's home.

He did not know whether Anna still lived. And, if so, where? Kiev, perhaps? She might still be there. Under the bridges. By the railway lines with a bottle in her hand. Maybe with a child, with a home. Maybe working in a shop. Maybe all or none of those things.

He did not dwell on it overly much. Though vague dreams of finding her again were a compass in his gut.

• • •

Poor wretched Magda.

That constant tugging and pulling and cracking and bending and not knowing and knowing.

Oh! It is unwise to try to make a window of Crow's heart, Magda.

Or any man's.

Or woman's either.

And so we let her follow him. Like on that other night. With nothing said and not much understood. Trailing behind him, deep and weary in the virgin snow.

23

A man—Callum Gourty was his name—came in through the door of a low, stone-built farmhouse with a pile of firewood in his arms. He knelt down and began to chock stack the logs beside a stove.

"I'm going over to Rathged tomorrow, Mum. See how they're getting on. You want to come?"

"Bethan'll be back soon, won't she?"

"And?"

"I've got eyes in my head, Callum," his mother said. "A man doesn't pretend *not* to see a pretty woman unless he's keen on her."

Callum laughed. "Hard to remember what she looks like." He threw a few logs onto the fire. The burning heat reddening his face.

Mrs. Gourty lowered herself into an armchair. "Well, I remember what you were like when she was here last summer. By the way, we're near out of sugar. And salt. When's the supply truck coming down to the Dolgellau base?"

"Tomorrow. I'm getting some things for Bran and Anwen too."

"Well, let's hope the worst of the weather has passed us by now."

"Huw Thomas came by this morning," Callum said. "Lost some sheep in the storm. Trying to get the carcasses out of the snow before the ravens pick them to pieces. He bought a new pony off me for the job."

"Did he pay good money? There are no flies on Huw Thomas."

"Said he'd pay in spring when the sheep go on the boat to Liverpool."

"Well, don't forget we'll be needing more candles," said Mrs. Gourty, sitting back in the chair.

Callum stood up from the fire and lugged a saddle onto the kitchen table. There was a pot of grease and a rag, and he began wiping the sweat and hairs from the padding on the underside, then pulled off the stirrup leathers and undid the buckles.

"So you'll come with me to Rathged tomorrow then, Mum?" he said, turning the saddle over.

"Of course I will. It'd be good to see Anwen and Alice." Mrs. Gourty rubbed her thick knees. Stared into the fire. "Anwen's as capable as anyone, but she's getting on. I worry about her. Loves that child more than her own self. It's a hard job for an old woman."

"You shouldn't worry so much, Mum—just fetch the sloe gin from the cupboard."

"Wouldn't mind seeing the first snowdrops sticking their silly heads out of the snow either. Could take them down to the church in Dolgellau. For Dad."

"You stay there. I'll get you a glass. Snowdrops will be out soon enough. Don't worry about that."

Callum put down his rag and wiped his hands on his trousers. He made his way across the brick floor of the low kitchen and opened the simple cross-braced door to the larder. They had enough supplies for a while yet: onions, flour, pasta, some long-life milk, the big hare he'd shot hanging from the hook. And high up on the shelf was the sloe gin. He took it down.

What would happen if Mum got ill? Really ill. He thought about what Huw Thomas had said—sitting over the table yesterday morning—talking in his gravelly Welsh voice.

"Oil's at seven hundred a barrel now, Gourty. Seven hundred! Can't afford to be buying any diesel next winter. Maybe just keep enough by for the generator. You could probably make a fortune selling your ponies, good hardy Welsh ponies like you've got. People will need them if it carries on like this. But your mother isn't getting any younger, is she. Maybe you should think about moving to the city. It's no good lifting your petticoats *after* pissing, is it? Now. Money for the pony in spring. That a deal then, Gourty?"

Callum smiled to himself and poured the glass of sloe gin for his mother.

"Do you hear that noise, Callum?" she said from the chair.

He handed her the drink.

"What?"

"That—"

A low drone in the sky outside. Growing louder.

He strode quickly to the front door, opened it up, and stepped out on the porch. Dusk was approaching. The sinking sun coloring the old stones of the house. The horizon was streaked with long mossy clouds, and the last light cast shadows on the snow-covered hill that fell down to the woods beyond the barn.

Callum looked up. The droning was almost overhead now. A crow rose, startled from the treetops, dark wings hauling it skyward for a moment, then it tumbled low and out of sight.

And then they passed. Two large army cargo planes, stout gray fuselages looming over the trees on the hillside. A pony neighed in fright on the other side of the barnyard.

The roaring passed over. His mother clutched at his side.

"Look. They're dropping something out of the back!"

She was right. Large bale-like bundles dropped from the rear They watched the droning planes disappear over the white peaks of Cader Idris, far away to the west.

"You best ride down to the base tomorrow and find out. Before we go over to Rathged. Aye, that's a good idea. Now let's get this door shut. You're letting out all the heat. And you need to feed the ponies."

"I know, Mum, I know." And Callum Gourty stuck his feet into his Wellingtons and tramped across the yard to the hay barn. Thinking about it all.

It's no good lifting your petticoats after *pissing, is it?*

He lifted a bale onto the wheelbarrow, the twine cutting into his palms. *Maybe take a boat trip up to Liverpool come the spring, sell some ponies.* He threw the hay over the rails. Leaned over the stable door. Rubbed a few warm noses in the darkness. Smelled the pony smell rising up from the deep litter of the barn.

Soon as the weather cleared. Go and have a sniff about town. Think about what Huw Thomas had said. Maybe it was madness—staying out here all winter.

"Callum"—there was a shout from the house. "Callum, it's the news on the radio. Get in quick if you don't want to miss it."

Mum using up the batteries again. Still, at least there was a signal.

He made his way back across the darkened barnyard to the house—boots crunching in the snow.

Yes, a lot to think about.

• • •

"Well. Charles is dead." Mrs. Gourty shifted in her seat. "Suppose it'll be William's turn now. Can't see how they're going to have much of a coronation with all the trouble though."

Callum sat opposite her in the high-backed wooden chair, his socked feet stretched out by the fire.

"It's the least of our worries if they've started shooting people on the streets—"

"Do you think they'll send the trucks to Dolgellau if they close the wind farm? What will we do if that stops? It's our lifeline in the winter. Barmouth's so far.'

They were quiet as a log fell in the fire. The glowing cubes of charcoal slumping in the grate.

"Maybe we should think of getting out. Going to Liverpool," said Callum. "Or Manchester. Soon as spring comes."

His mother was very still. She looked over at her son. Not made to be stuck in the city.

"Can't leave the ponies, Callum," she said with a firm smile. "I'm as fit as I've ever been. It'll be spring soon. And all this nonsense will die down. It's only a bad winter."

Callum looked at her. "Ten bad winters, Mum."

But she saw that he wanted to believe her.

24

Frozen to the marrow from hours of wading through knee-deep snow, Magda slid down a steep verge between a line of rotten ash trees. She fell, tumbling in a long disused runnel.

Ivan helped her up, wind whipping the flaps of his coat.

"I can't feel my feet anymore," she said, teeth chattering.

He pulled her close. Shouted above the wind: "There are some trees. It is not far. Look. Under the hill. We will stop in there."

He helped her through the drifts and grabbed at branches in the hedgerow on the other side of the track, pulling her across a shallow-ditched verge.

A dark woodland spiked far off against the white. On they crept, strength fading, cheeks stinging with cold. The hard boots of the boy from the park rubbed at her frozen, blistered feet. Would Ivan never let her rest?

They stopped at last in the fringes of the wood, floundered under the lee of the trees, branches whipping ominously above.

Magda pulled the matches from her pocket, barely able to feel her fingers. "We must light a fire. I don't care who sees it."

"Not yet," he said, taking the matches gently from her hand.

"Please. I can't go any further."

But Ivan trudged ahead into the branch-fingered dimness.

An old stone wall poked out of the snow. He climbed over it onto a track between the tree trunks. Two weather-beaten posts loomed in the darkness. He approached them and peered up at the snow-spattered name carved upon the old gray stone.

RATHGED FARM

He passed between the gateposts, his lone figure a small, dark shadow against the white. Something swept up through the trees. A whir of wings.

And he saw ahead of him, against a gentle hill, the woodland had been cleared. And there it stood.

A house.

Faint light at a window.

He watched it for some time, then turned and hurried back under the trees.

"Magda, get up. There is a house."

• • •

Rathged Farm was low and rambling. It had been built from stone blocks laid deep in the walls and dressed neat around windows and doors. A solid bulwark against the incessant winds and soaking Welsh rains. Outhouses were tumbled at one end of the building in an odd mishmash of weathered oak lintels and stepped slate roofs that clearly ran around the back of the dwelling to some sort of yard.

Save for the addition of a corrugated-tin porch, the house itself was in no way eccentric, with small, square windows and thick barred panes, the upper ones scowling like dark eyes under mean eaves. It was a house that had built itself of the landscape and a long tradition of restraint that brooked no decorative overhang or ceiling higher than a man might need to stand under. No slate had been split or timber sawn to please man's eye. *Just get the house up quick. But warmth you must have*—and narrow chimneys poked up from each end of a snow-rounded roof. From one of these broken chimney pots came a dribble of smoke, beaten every which way by the howling wind that cut and tumbled from the hillside.

Magda and Ivan came closer. The hint of a light glowed behind a dirty windowpane, overgrown rhododendrons thrashed around the door and rattled on the porch. Ivan lifted the knocker, and with one quick glance at Magda he rapped three times.

• • •

The muffled sound of barking.

A wait in the tumbling snow.

A pulling back of bolts.

It was a man who opened the door: an old man, and not too tall. But he was not frail. Not a bit of it. Thick homemade socks were pulled over his patched trousers, the fronts of which were worn to a sheen. A bulky sweater, darned at both cuffs, frayed over his hands—and to complete the look of dishevelment, a pair of heavy-soled slippers anchored him to the doormat.

There was a dog—evidently the source of the barking, wheezing now as its tail slapped at the old man's legs. It was a portly, ancient collie, pulling back its lip out of habit.

"What do you want?" the old man grunted, hanging back suspiciously in his dark porch. Then the man saw. Without a word he let the strangers inside and closed the door firmly behind them. As they squeezed into a dingy hallway, the smell of house—a strange new smell, of other people, and dog, and wood, and cloth, and plaster; a sharp, slightly pungent smell, and not altogether pleasant—flooded their senses.

Dirty wellies and slippers spilled out onto a worn rug by the door; coats, hats, waterproof capes, and bulky sweaters hung several to a hook on the wall. An old woman peered from the dimness of the hallway, curling gray hair framing her face.

The man picked up a candlestick from among a collection of ceramic dogs neatly arranged on a small table. He held the flickering light up.

"Where the bloody hell have you two come from then?"

Magda's head swam. Blood sank to her feet. A sound like water in her ears.

"Bran," the old woman cried out, "Bran. Quick. The girl's falling—"

• • •

With candlelight guttering on the whitewashed walls, Ivan followed the beckoning hands up the creaking stairs.

• • •

A door was opened. Voices talked in hushed whispers. But Magda barely heard them. Let herself be laid on a bed.

"Babula?"

The spirits from the forest crept up.

She felt them on her chest. Could feel the sharpness of their fingers pricking her clothing.

Why did you leave the village?

Ha! Put your left shoe on your right foot and your right shoe on your left foot—

Brunon? Brunon Dudek?

A terror filled her. Her eyes would not open. Her hand could not move.

She was awake, but knew she was dreaming. Wanted the dream to stop. But still her arm would not move.

It lay cold on the snow.

So cold.

She felt Crow's hard claws on her chest. Her fingers twitched.

Crow screeched, wings beating around her face, feathers scratching her skin. It cawed again.

"No invite, bitch."

The crow no longer a crow.

That grimacing mouth, breathing on her. It held up broken fingers. Laughed.

"We're gonna have a little tumble—"

She saw it now. That startled lifeless face in the snow. Yes—it was a lifeless face, blood at the ear where her blow had struck.

She struggled. Lashed out with her arms.

• • •

"Magda—wake up, it's just a dream."

There was a gentle shuffling of clothes, she felt her boots

being taken off and warm hands on her feet; the pulling over of blankets, the sound of the door being closed.

"Ivan—"

Half-parted curtains at a window. Snow battering outside them. A figure pulling them shut. The glow of a candle beside the bed, flickering in the draft.

"Ivan? Is it you?"

"Yes."

"What happened?"

"You fainted."

He sat beside her, a weight on the edge of the mattress. The thump of boots hitting the floor. And he climbed into the bed; she could smell him, smoke on his hair, on his clothes. That other smell: his smell.

"Drink this." He handed her a cup of something warm, and she drank.

"Where are we?"

"I don't know, some old people."

"I think I killed him, Ivan."

"What?"

"The boy. In the park."

"Which boy?"

"The one who tried to—I hit him. His face was so still."

She felt Ivan's hand in her hair and sucked the tenderness up like parched earth. His hand remained. Everything in her converged on the feel of his touch.

"Sleep, Magda. Sleep."

"Are we safe?"

"Yes." He took her cup and snuffed out the candle with his fingers. He lay there waiting for her to fall asleep, listening to the night sounds of the strange house. Alert as an owl.

. . .

Downstairs, Bran Mortimer scuffed across the floor in those ratty slippers with that old dog blustering at his side. He chided it good-naturedly, stopped to wind a plain-fronted grandfather clock, then opened a door into a small kitchen, with worn black and red tiles on the floor and a fug in the air from a pan of oats simmering on an Aga.

Bran scraped a chair back from under the table. His wife, Anwen, shuffled in from the back porch and threw a sturdy armful of split logs into the stove, a cloud of smoke puffing up into the room as the cast-iron hob plate rattled back into place. She took the oats off the boil and bent down to put the pan in the slow oven for the night. She riddled the Aga, then heaved herself up and settled herself opposite her husband in a creaking wooden chair.

Anwen Mortimer was a woman who had grown a little thickset with age. It was not that she was overfed or underworked, nor ever had been, but having spent most of her life halfway content she had grown stouter, not thinner, with age. And since she had not only climbed the stairs three times this night but also fetched blankets and warmed precious milk, removed boots and puzzled over foreign tongues whispering—and been so generally intrigued by the strange arrival of two frozen foreigners coming in from the wild night—she was now utterly out of breath. And full of questions.

"Do you think it's safe having them in the house?" she said to her husband. "We don't know who they are. Or where they're from."

"We'll find out more in the morning."

"Did you see the girl's feet when I took off her boots? Terrible."

"I did."

"Well, it's not normal." She swiped at nonexistent crumbs on the well-wiped Formica. "Do you think they'll be all right up there with no fire?"

"They're young. I dare say it'll be warmer up there than it would have been if they were stuck outside tonight."

"The boy sounded Russian, didn't he?"

"Perhaps," said her husband. "Maybe they followed the army track from the road. Got lost."

"But that's miles away," Anwen said. She got up, snuffed out the lamp hanging from the ceiling, and took the candle from the table. "I must say, it's all very odd."

"Well, there's nothing we can do about it now."

Bran followed her down the passageway into the front room. He sat on the bed that was pushed into the corner and pulled off his socks. He let his wife's wittering wash over him like the snow-flakes gusting against the panes:

Three more sheep lame. And no more diesel. Not a word from Bethan since her letter in November. And if ANPEC aban-doned the Cefn Coch wind farm they wouldn't keep the track to the main road clear and they wouldn't have the army supply store in Dolgellau. Thank God for Callum Gourty lending a hand now and then. Thank God it was nearly spring. Thank God for that at least.

Anwen crept to the sofa. Under a bundle of blankets and rugs, a small child was sleeping, a hank of fine hair spilling over the pillow. The old lady peered down, stroked the child's hair and rearranged the bedding unnecessarily.

"Still fast asleep," she whispered, smiling.

The old couple undressed, pulling thick sleeping gowns over their vests and undergarments, and they lay close and still in the narrow bed, waiting for the cold sheets to warm beneath them.

The child murmured in its sleep.

"We should get down to Dolgellau, as soon as the weather clears—try and call Bethan," whispered Anwen. "Let her know Alice is well at least."

In the hallway, the dog raised its head. Looked toward the front door.

Something had fluttered and stirred.

But it was only an ill wind creeping over the threshold and the sound of snow gusting against windows and falling heavy on every roof.

25

The springs in the mattress creaked as Magda lifted herself up from the pillow.

An early light slanted across the floorboards, brightening the faded color on some ancient threadbare rug and spilling up onto the thick quilt that lay heavy across her body.

There was the sound of a child somewhere downstairs, the running of feet and a door closing.

A child? Here?

She pulled back the bedclothes and looked down at her blistered feet, slid down, padded across the cold floor, and looked out the window

What time is it? And where is Ivan?

She rubbed at the frozen condensation on the pane. Outside, the sky was clear, casting green-blue shadows on a newborn landscape that stretched away as far as she could see. The woods surrounding the house were still and bare, a patchwork of white fields and tree-covered foothills in the distance.

And from the woodland a man emerged, leading a pony with an old woman seated on its back. The figures made their way toward the house, kicking up a trail in the new snow. As he came through the gate, the man caught sight of Magda at the window.

He smiled up and raised a hand as if he knew her, then realized that he did not, and looked away.

Magda stepped back behind the curtain.

There was a knock on the bedroom door.

"Are you up yet?" The handle turned and the old lady appeared. "I've got you some fresh clothes. And hot water." She pushed the door open with her elbow, huffing breathlessly, and struggled in with a bowl of steaming water. Magda took it from her hands, and the old lady dipped back out of the door, only to reappear moments later with a jug, some soap, a towel, and a bundle of clothes.

"You'll feel better after a wash." She plumped the clothes down on the bed and sat down to catch her breath. "I don't know what would have happened if you'd been out in the weather last night."

"Where is my . . . my friend?" said Magda.

"He's gone to cut some firewood with my husband. They'll be back later. Your boots are drying in the kitchen. When you're ready, come down."

"It is very kind of you to let us stay here—"

"Oh, don't worry about that." The old woman got up from the chair. "And I'm Anwen." She looked a little embarrassed. "I thought you might start talking a lot of gibberish like your friend."

"His name is Ivan; I am Magda." Magda smiled. "From Poland. He doesn't speak English really."

"Poland, is it. Poland, eh. Should have guessed." She patted the pile of clothes. "They're my daughter Bethan's clothes. This is her room."

"She is not here?"

"No. Her little girl Alice lives with us though. You'll meet her when you come down."

Magda stood awkwardly on the thin rug.

"Well, I'll let you be." Anwen gave a quick smile and went out, closing the door gently behind her.

Magda listened to her heavy tread descending the stair. Stuck to the back of the door was a poster of three slick-haired boys— The Razors. The daughter's bedroom. The ceilings were low and the floors were dusty—every corner laced with last year's cobwebs. She could feel grit on the rug. Aside from the high bed, there was a narrow chest for clothes and a small iron fireplace, which had been boarded up.

She locked the door and knelt down. Took off her shirt and splashed steaming water onto her face. She hung her long hair into the bowl, and using the soap she raised a lather, pouring the last water from the jug to rinse. Afterward, with the water gray and scummy, she washed the dry blood from her feet, rubbed herself down with the towel, and with splayed fingers combed through the tangles in her hair.

Her old clothes lay in a pile on the floor, gray and worn and dirty. The new clothes folded on the bed smelled of camphor: a pair of pants, thick woolen socks that only needed a little darning at the heel, a vest, a shirt and sweater, a pair of trousers, and even shoes. She put the new things on, which felt very good, gathered her own dirty clothes under one arm, and went out onto the landing. She found her way down the dim staircase, following the sound of voices to the kitchen.

• • •

There was another woman at the kitchen table. She stopped talking as Magda opened the door.

"Magda. Come and sit by the Aga. Dry your hair," said Anwen, standing at a sink, peeling turnips. "This," she said, waving a hand toward the woman at the table, "is Mrs. Gourty, our neighbor." She turned to Mrs. Gourty. "Magda and her friend Ivan turned up in the night."

"In the night? What on earth were they doing wandering about in this weather?" said Mrs. Gourty.

There was a small girl scrubbing at a scrap of paper with an orange crayon. Shoulder-length brown hair fell over her face as she worked. She looked up and gave Magda a glance. *"Dydy hi'n andros o denau, Nain—"**

"Shh, Alice!" said Anwen, with her hand on the little girl's shoulder, the hardened knuckles like Babula's. "This is my granddaughter. Alice."

"Hello," said Magda.

The little girl stared. "You sound funny." She continued her scrubbing.

"Here, give me those." Anwen took the bundle of dirty clothes from Magda's arms. She turned to Mrs. Gourty. "She's from Poland, Fiona."

---

* "She's right thin, Granny—"

208

"Poland! What on earth are you doing here then?" said Mrs. Gourty.

With a stamping of boots, the back door opened and her son Callum came into the kitchen.

"Here are the things you wanted from Dolgellau, Anwen," he said, putting a bag on the table.

Anwen riffled about in the bag and took out a packet of tea.

Callum pulled out a chair and sat down at the table.

"I'll fetch you something," said Anwen, going to the Aga. She filled the kettle with water from a jug and put it to boil.

"Who's this?" Callum waved his hand at Magda.

"Her name's Magda. Found her out on the step last night. From Poland."

"Mmm. And that boy in the log shed with Bran—him too?"

"Yes. They're friends." Anwen brought a bowl of porridge to the table. Callum Gourty put his hat down and pushed his coat off onto the back of his chair. He looked at Magda. "You speak English?"

"I learn in school."

"Long way from Poland."

"I came to find my mother."

"Here?" he said.

"No, London."

"I take it you didn't."

"No."

"Why here then?"

"We have car, but a man steal it and leave us on the road. We are trying to go to Liverpool."

"Liverpool? Boat doesn't run in winter."

"Boat? I do not know of a boat," said Magda. "But we have a friend there who will help us go home."

"You came here from London then?"

Magda hesitated, then nodded.

"No place for city people out here. But I guess you've already found that out." He took a spoonful of porridge. Eyes steady as a sniper, watching her across the table like a hawk.

"I am not from city," said Magda. "I come from village—we have horses and cows and sheep, and Bogdan Stopko had tractor and two fields."

Callum laughed. "Did he now."

"We have much snow on mountain, like here in England."

"And you left Poland to find your mother."

"She had a job in London. My grandmother die and the people from my village were taken away by soldiers. I hide in cellar so they cannot find me, but I ride across the hill and find another village and I go in the trucks to Krakow. With my friend. Ivan."

Callum put his spoon down.

"Why did they take you away from your village?"

"Weather very bad in Poland," Magda said. "They take villagers to the city. I hear president on radio. He say it is Emergency."

"State of Emergency." Mrs. Gourty nodded. "Heard that on the radio. Here too as well."

Callum leaned back in his chair and raised an eyebrow at Anwen. "Met some soldiers this morning, on the Dolgellau road.

Asked if I'd seen two Polish kids. Said they'd probably be pilfering someone's bins."

"Soldiers say they will take us to police—" blurted Magda.

"Why?"

"We have no papers."

Anwen and Mrs. Gourty exchanged a *look*.

Magda saw it. "We hurt no one. We only want to go home. We have a friend. In Liverpool—"

"Well, you're in Wales now, girl. And you won't be getting up to Liverpool for a bit. Does that boy come from your village too?"

"No. He comes from Ukraine. It is long way."

"The Ukraine!" exclaimed Anwen.

"So you're both stuck," Callum said.

Magda was silent and looked down at her hands. She did not know why she had told them so many things.

There was a rattling of a door and old Bran Mortimer came in through his back door. "Morning, all," he said, putting his boots to dry at the back of the Aga. He peered down at his granddaughter's scrawling. "So, what's the road to Dolgellau like, Callum?"

"It'll clear. You'd get down there easy enough with the tractor this afternoon."

"Where's that foreign boy?" asked Anwen.

"He's still splitting logs, and it's good to see someone young and fit doing the work for a change."

"They're illegals," said his wife, folding her arms across her chest.

"What?"

"We've been having a chat with the girl," said Callum, gesturing with his thumb at Magda.

"What if the army come round here asking questions?" Anwen said. "What do we do then, I ask you?"

Mrs. Gourty stood up and pulled on a large duffel coat. "What can you do? It's miles across country and the Liverpool boat won't come until spring." She buttoned her toggles and pulled a knitted hat from her pocket. "Anyway, they can't go wandering about the countryside in this kind of weather."

"Bet she's quite handy with animals and all that," Callum said. "Country girl like her. And the boy—there's more wood needs chopping, isn't there, Bran? Fences to be laid. You could use a strong pair of hands, help in the house. And there's work up at our place too."

"But what if soldiers come round asking?" said Bran. "What should we do then?"

"They've got enough on their plates without bothering about two kids. Don't worry. You won't be the only farm to have a few Poles mending the roof this winter."

Bran rubbed at his scratchy gray stubble. "Can't pack them off in the snow right away anyhow."

Mrs. Gourty wriggled plump hands into her gloves. "No. Well, we've got ponies to feed." She leaned close to Anwen's ear. "And you can send Bethan up to our place as soon as she gets back in the spring. Callum gets bored of my company."

"Mum." Callum reddened under his beard and ushered his

mother out the door. Their heavy-coated backs disappeared into the back porch.

Out in the snow-filled yard, Callum untied the pony. "Why did you say that about Bethan?"

"You can't just wait for apples to fall in your lap."

"Bethan Mortimer's not interested in me. Or she wouldn't have left Rathged."

"Well, it's very exciting having a couple of runaways out here."

"Bran's lucky. We could use a pair of hands with spring on its way. But there's something that girl's not telling us." He looped the rein over the pony's withers and helped his mother up into the saddle. He led the pony out of the yard and away under the trees, toward the river and their place on the other side of the hill.

From the kitchen window, Bran watched them plodding away in the snow. *Funny man, that Callum Gourty.*

Ivan came in from outside and laid an axe by the door. His face was red. Magda looked up at him. She had said too much and she was certain he would be angry. It had all unraveled like a ball of wool.

"They know about the soldiers," she said.

For a moment he was still, then he took her by the elbow. "Let's go. Get your things."

"Not so fast, lad," said the old man, his hand on Ivan's shoulder.

"We will leave," Magda said. "We do not want to cause any trouble."

The little girl looked up. "Are they going to go away?"

Anwen, flustered, swiveled to the hob. She wrapped a towel over the handle, lifted it clear, and filled a large teapot on the sideboard.

"Please don't make them go," said Alice. "She's too thin to go away, Granny."

"Well, first off, let's all have a cup of tea," said Anwen. "They've spent a night under our roof, Bran, and they'll have a bite to eat, even if I have to break a spade over the boy's head. That girl isn't being dragged out in the snow yet. For a start, she's wearing Bethan's clothes."

"Well, there's no point telling it to me—" Bran tipped his head at Magda and Ivan, whispering at the end of the table. "They look more like two hares about to take flight than birds settling down to nest."

"Right then, you two," said Anwen—loud and matter-of-fact.

Magda and Ivan looked up as one, startled.

"Before you get too hasty," Anwen said, "let's have some tea." She held the large teapot like an offering. "Tea, and a chat about what we're all going to do."

26

Magda and Ivan followed the old couple down a disused passage-way with Alice skipping about at their feet. At the end of it was a low wooden door.

"Right—" Anwen pushed at it. "Haven't—been"—she gave it a hearty shove with her hip—"in here for a while." The swollen boards scraped across an uneven flagstone floor. Alice scooted around her grandmother's legs and peered into the room. It was dark inside, and smelled of damp—a grayness falling in between cracks at a boarded window.

"You'll have to go outside and pull the boards off, Bran. Let in some light."

"I'll fetch a hammer," he said. "Come on, Ivan."

"I think it's going to have lots of spiders," said Alice, climbing up on one of the wobbly chairs at a small pine table.

"It's the old farm kitchen," said Anwen. "Been boarded up for years." Her breath misted the cold air. "There's a range—it's an old thing but"—she stepped around a stack of rotting tea chests and mice-eaten cardboard boxes—"should work."

Outside, there was a creaking, as first one board, then another, was jimmied away from the snow-piled window. Ivan looked in through the dirty glass, and when he had pulled the last plank away from the window frame, the room was flooded with the cold light.

"There *are* lots of cobwebs, Nain!" cried Alice.

"Well, there won't be too many flies then, will there?" Anwen tugged at the oven and the rusty door creaked open on heavy hinges. She swiped at the cobwebs. "The whole place needs a good clean. Oh, there's a larder too." She lifted the latch on a narrow door, the dusty shelves inside lined with red-and-white-checked plastic. "The larder always used to be chock-full of jams and preserves and a big homemade cheese or two when I first came to Rathged. Bran's mother was still alive then," she said. "And here's a door into the back garden." She pulled aside a mildewed curtain and rattled the bolts. "Need to unlock it from outside. Like I said, all the place needs is a good clean and a fire to dry up the damp. There's a small bedroom upstairs."

"Can I see?" Magda asked.

"Of course."

A narrow, worm-eaten staircase led up to a tiny landing. The bedroom had stained black floorboards and faded rose-spray wallpaper peeling at the edges. A metal bed frame was pushed against the wall, the striped mattress beyond repair, clumps of stuffing falling out where small creatures had ransacked it for bedding of their own. There was a small fire grate and a narrow mantelpiece. And in the corner a folding wooden clothes rail and old-fashioned tin bathtub with enameled handles.

Magda went to the window. There were dead flies on the sill

and cobwebs as thick as lace. She pulled back a faded curtain and rubbed at the glass.

Down below was an orchard all bare and frosted, a spiky hedge and a squat stone wall bounding the low end of it, and rising up to the right was the stable block and a narrow gate leading to the yard behind the main house.

Puffing and creaking, Anwen twisted herself up the narrow stairs. "What do you think then? Spot of work about the farm and it's all yours."

Magda turned silently back to the window and the trees outside. She tried to imagine them in leaf, heavy with apples, birds singing in the hedge, the grass new and green. "And we can have firewood? And maybe some blankets and things for the kitchen?"

"Yes," said Anwen, looking around the bare and dusty room. "We could find another mattress for the bed and you can burn all the boxes out in the orchard. There's nothing in them that will be any good anymore."

Ivan poked his head through the door.

"We can stay here, Ivan," Magda said. "All we need to do is work a little on the farm..."

He saw her bright face. "Yes. We will stay. Until the weather clears."

• • •

They threw the old boxes and tea chests onto a bonfire out in the orchard. Alice stood in the doorway, mesmerized by the shooting flames leaping out over the snow. Finally, Ivan hauled the lumpy cotton-filled mattress from the bed and pushed it down the stairs.

"One, two, three—" They swung it onto the top of the fire and waited for it to catch. Anwen gathered up a box of spare pots and pans and brushes and cloths from her own kitchen, and rattled them down on the table.

Magda hauled two buckets of water from the house and put them, sloshing, on the kitchen floor.

Ivan wheeled several loads of firewood from the log shed and began to stack them in the lean-to by the back door. Magda cleaned the ash in the range and laid a bed of twigs and old paper in the grate.

"We could probably do with cleaning the chimney," said Bran, watching her. "But I'm sure it'll do for now."

Alice came pushing past his legs and peered in at all the bustle. Anwen too poked her head around the door. "I'll give you a bit of help if you want it."

"No," said Magda cheerfully. "Thank you. I will do it myself. You have your own work. And when I have finished I will come and take my clothes to wash, and if you have anything for me to do . . ."

Anwen nudged Bran. "See," she whispered in his ear. "Gourty was right. I think we'll get on very well with them."

• • •

Magda's knees ached as she knelt on the flagstones and cleaned the range with a wire brush. As she worked, clouds of rust came floating from where she scrubbed. Ivan gave the window a shove.

Cold air welled into the room, gusting out through the back door. Magda looked about at the bare, dirty, dusty, freezing, cobwebbed room. "It will be good when it is clean," she said.

Ivan smiled, watching her wrap a cloth around her hair. Perhaps it was her certainty that he liked.

"What?" she said, hands above her head tying the knot.

"Nothing. Just you, Havemercy."

"Don't you have logs to stack?" She picked up the broom.

• • •

It was a hard bit of effort sweeping around the old beams in the ceiling, with the broom snagging on hooks and nails, and her hands in the air the whole time. Ivan came in and laughed, and she said, "*Stop laughing.*" So he took the broom and made a passable job of the room upstairs to save her aching arms.

Then she made him carry the table out into the snow, and the heavy oak dresser too so she could clean the floor.

"Who are you expecting?" he said.

"You want to sleep in a sty?" She knelt down and lit the fire in the grate. She tipped her head to one side and peered into the oven. The twigs had caught and so she fetched some logs and put them in with a billowing cloud of smoke that made her cough. Then she closed the window and filled the copper with water and an arc of warmth began to spread out across the room.

"Ivan—"

But Ivan had sneaked to the orchard to poke meaningfully at the remains of the bonfire with a smile across his face.

• • •

When Anwen came in to announce that there was food ready, she was not prepared for the change that Magda had wrought in the old kitchen. She opened the door to a warm and spotless room, bare indeed, but her old pans arranged neatly on the shelf, the sink scrubbed clean, the floor damp in the corners but drying from where it had been washed.

A neat stack of logs had been piled beside the range and Magda sweated over the pine table with a stiff scrubbing brush.

Clomping sounds from upstairs suggested that the boy, Ivan, was busy in the bedroom, and Anwen was satisfied that these two strangers were indeed *a good bet*. It was a shame, she could not help thinking, to be burning another fire in the house, but that was unavoidable.

"Here's something to eat," she said, putting a pot on the table. "And I must say you've made a thorough job of this place, Magda. It's all very cozy. In the morning we'll see what jobs need doing about the farm if you're feeling well enough for it. Well—" She looked about one more time with a satisfied gaze. "Goodnight."

Anwen closed the door. They heard Alice twittering on down the passageway, and the dog gave a bark from the depths of the house. Finally, a door closed far off and Magda hurried up the stairs to the bedroom.

"There is food, Ivan—"

Ivan was kneeling on the floor by the bed. His coat lay beside him, the bundle of illegal passports and the wedge of remaining zloty in a pile on top of it. He was prizing up a floorboard with a piece of metal.

Carefully, he laid the passports and money between the joists and put the floorboard back in place, hammering the nails in over a cloth to deaden the sound.

He looked up at Magda. "Until the weather clears."

• • •

After they had eaten, Magda lit a candle on the mantelpiece. Outside, the snow had stopped falling and the wind had died and there was a quiet peace. She fetched an armful of logs from the shed and shut the door. Just the small dark window was an ominous black eye in the room, and she hung a cloth over it.

"You have made a good job of this place," Ivan said, coming up close behind her as she stretched up on her toes to hook the cloth over a nail. He rested his chin on her shoulder and crept his hands about her waist. "Must be time for bed . . ."

"I don't know why the English do not have shutters," Magda said, taking his hands from her waist. "Every room is like being naked."

Ivan sauntered back to the fire and stretched his arms in the air. Dropping them suddenly, he clomped up the narrow stairs, three steps at a time, and came down, clanging the old tin bathtub against the walls. "Let's wash."

She dipped her chin at him.

"Why not?" He grinned.

So they scraped the tub down on the floor by the fire and filled it with hot water from the range, bucket by slow bucket.

It seemed to Magda that this was a very pleasant thing to be doing. They laughed a bit and water spilled on the flagstones. She hung two small towels on the back of a chair to warm.

It was all ready.

"You first," Ivan said.

A very pleasant thing to be doing until you have done it and the bath sits there waiting for you to be naked.

She blushed.

"I'll sit at the table and promise not to look." Ivan put his hand in front of his eyes, then he opened his fingers like bars in a cage, and looked through them, grinning at her. "I promise."

Magda slapped at him playfully, her cheeks red.

"All right, all right—I'll go upstairs."

When she heard him creaking on the floor above, Magda finally undressed.

"Don't you dare come down," she shouted at the ceiling.

She stood bare. Her clothes folded on the chair. Her feet flat on the cold stone floor.

So this is what it is to be naked with a man so near.

She tucked her long pale hair into a roll at the nape of her neck, flicked a nervous look at the door, and stepped into the water.

It felt very hot. The water stung her blistered feet. She stood in it for several moments then lowered herself down, the tin sides cold against her arms.

A wave of homesickness came over her then. A strange sense of unease. She felt uncovered, unprotected in some way she could not reconcile. Like a sparrow in a gale. Blown every which way and unable to land.

And it was not just the nakedness. And the thought of the one mattress upstairs.

There were footsteps from above.

You have made your own bed, even if you did not have much choice. Now you must lie in it.

She swirled the water with her hand; the heat dissipated a little.

And how lucky you are to have a bed for the night.

She wiped the perspiration from her neck. The water felt good.

She held her fingers up in front of her eyes like Ivan had done, and looked through them. She laughed quietly because it *was* quite funny, and then she relaxed, and her head tipped back and she rested her arms on the edges of the tub where the handles formed a ledge and her hair fell out of the twist at her neck and slumped into the water and she closed her eyes and listened to the spitting of the fire in the range for a while, and felt the first gentle warmth for a long time, creeping into her bones.

And so, like that, she pretended neither to hear Ivan's tread on the stair—nor his turning of the door handle.

And Ivan came over and put his hand in her damp hair. She opened her eyes. And he kissed her.

It wasn't so difficult after all.

And they went upstairs.

Sparrows in the gale.

27

"Out the way, Daffodil!" Anwen pushed a hairy ginger sow away and emptied a bucket of oats and scraps into the trough. "Ivor there is far better behaved."

A large boar snouted over and snuffled his nose about in the feed. Anwen scratched at his back and he flicked his short curly tail and grunted.

"You muck this lot out," Anwen said, "and then we'll do the cows. Don't let Daffodil near the gate. She's a runner, and if she gets a sniff of freedom we'll be an hour getting her back in. Don't be mean with the straw either; they only eat more if they're cold." She held the stable door open and Magda pushed the wheelbarrow into the sty. She rubbed at the sow's ear. It grunted happily, chomping on a turnip end.

"If we're lucky, she'll have a good litter this year—enough that we can slaughter a few to sell in Dolgellau."

"Is the town near?" said Magda.

"Town!" Anwen scoffed. "A village at best. And there's nothing there except the army store. Some people come back in the summer thinking they can raise some chickens and grow a few cabbages. There's a market then of course. And plenty of traders come on the Liverpool boat to pay low-down prices to us who've been working all year in the snow."

"The boat—is it the only way to Liverpool? Even in the spring?"

"Pretty much, since the roads have been so bad and fuel so expensive. And electric cars don't help when the lines are always down. Not that we ever had any newfangled cars out here."

"Does the boat come often?"

"Every couple of weeks to the fish market at Barmouth. People get down the river to Dolgellau from there. There are still a few of us out here with things to sell. And I'd like to see someone try to stop us. There's Huw Thomas and his family over the hill: he still has his sheep. And you've met the Gourtys: they've got the ponies, although there's no trekking business anymore, and— Daffodil! Get. Off!" Anwen pushed the sow away with her knee and slammed the sty door shut. "Well, I'd better feed the chickens and let you get on. And watch out for that pig!"

Ivan came over with a bale of straw from the barn at the end of the farmyard.

Three cows hung shaggy heads over a rail, clouds of warm breath snorting from wet noses. They were short-legged, black-haired beasts, not a sort that Magda had seen before, and they watched her work with a herdlike interest as she shoveled pig shit into her wheelbarrow.

Ivan leaned over the door. "They've got us working soon enough."

Magda stabbed her fork into the dung in the barrow and smiled. "'Us'?"

"I've been splitting logs for the last two hours. You should see my hands—" He held them out.

Magda went to him and held them, turned them over gently. Then she reached over the gate and kissed him on the cheek. "Poor thing." She laughed. "Hey," she added. "Throw the straw over before you go."

Ivan hefted the bale onto the top of the stable door and she grabbed it and pulled it over to the back of the sty. Bending it against her knee she pulled off the twine and opened it up.

The pigs came over, grunting piggily as they wriggled their heads, tossing the loosened straw in the air.

Magda used this moment of distraction to open the gate and get the barrow out before Daffodil realized she had missed her chance of freedom.

Ivan grasped her arms. "Come here—" And he tried to kiss her. And not on the cheek either.

Magda pushed him off. "*Someone might be watching—*" and she hurried past him with the barrow. "Don't forget to put more logs on the stove," she said, without the backward glance that would show her red-cheeked smile.

• • •

Anwen came out from the chicken shed with Alice. The little girl slipped into the cow pen and pranced about on the clean straw.

Anwen hauled a bucket of water over the gate and Magda topped up the water troughs and filled the manger. The cows stretched up sturdy necks and pulled out wisps of hay, chewing slowly with the gastric rumblings and gentle lowing of feeding cattle.

"I usually come and give them a brushing if they've been in for a bit," said Anwen. "I like cows. They're gentle, pleasant animals on the whole. The two heifers there—that one's called Primrose, and the other, with the little horns showing, is May. The pregnant one is Queenie. Not very original names, I know. She'll be calving soon, Queenie will—look at her." She patted the cow's rump. "I hope the weather gets better in good time so we can let them out."

Animals in the barn, work to be done, fires to be lit, children to be fed. Life going on. But not in Morochov, thought Magda.

"Animals have simple ways," she said. "Sometimes I wish our own lives were so simple." She surprised herself with the words. They were Brunon Dudek's words. Where was Brunon now? And his brother Aleksy, and the Kowalskis and Stopko's dog? Was Bogdan Stopko still in Krakow even?

And Mama? Where was she?

"You must be wanting to know where your mother is, and wondering how you're going to get back to Poland," said Anwen, reading her thoughts.

"In the spring they will let the people go back to the villages," Magda said quietly. "I am sure. I will find her then."

"What if there's a war?"

"War?"

"They talk about it on the radio," Anwen said.

Magda turned to her. "Ivan says the same thing. Do you think it will happen?"

"Lord knows," said Anwen. "Maybe it's just talk—the radio people love to talk. These bad winters have made people silly. I shouldn't worry too much. You can get to Liverpool easily enough once the Barmouth boat's running again. Find your friend—the one who can help you. I'm sure you'll find your mother then."

They were silent for a moment.

"Why does your daughter not stay here?" said Magda. "Why has she gone away?"

"Oh, Bethan. She's earning money. For Alice."

"But why can you not make enough money selling milk and meat at the market? Your daughter could help you."

"Bethan's not interested in getting her hands covered in muck. Not interested in this life of being up every morning at five. Not interested in old clothes and rough hands."

"But what about the child's father? Where is he?"

Anwen turned her heavy-coated body—and the conversation—away from the stable door, and since Alice was pestering conveniently, she took the little girl's small hand in her plump one, and changed the subject.

"Come on, Magda. Time for a cup of tea! Let's get in and warm up a bit after all your good work. And you can soak your feet again. You don't want those blisters getting infected."

• • •

After lunch, Magda boiled a kettle and washed the pans in Anwen's kitchen. She found herself happy, with thoughts of being alone with Ivan in the little room last night. Ivan blowing out the candle and coming over—his body cold in the dark. It was as if the other things that had happened were a thousand miles away when he had kissed her and she had kissed him back—and more, and was not ashamed of it at last.

It was some kind of thrill that was entirely new and she smiled unthinkingly with it.

When she had finished the washing up, she dried her hands and looked about the room. *This place has got dirty round the edges with two old people on their own here. And a dog in the house.*

In Babula's cottage, every tiny thing had a place and a purpose. Everything was cherished. Cleaned and polished because it had been hard-won. *"Smoluch!"* the old women in the village would have muttered to one another about anyone with so much as a speck of dust on the shelves.

If Magda ever complained of boredom, Babula would have her cleaning the windows with old newspaper and vinegar.

"Make the most of what you've got, Magda. And be happy with it," Babula would say, knuckles red with scrubbing at sheets in the wooden tub.

• • •

You can put this place in order while you are here, thought Magda. *Make the most of it.* That was it. Putting something in order. Even if her own life was like a badly packed suitcase of mismatched shoes that had been thrown down a hill.

• • •

"When do you wash the sheets?" she asked Anwen.

"Sheets? Whenever I get the time. It's all got to be done by hand. I used to take the washing machine for granted, I can tell you."

Magda looked at the washing machine in the corner, piled with old magazines and a bag of chicken feed. Back in the village, Kowalski's wife had had a washing machine once. Brought by her son who worked in Germany.

"A washing machine, Mama," he announced proudly, dragging it out of the back of his car and attaching it with a pump to the well. The old villagers crowding around to watch.

But after he left, it had soon stopped working: the pump blocked with grit.

"Didn't get anything clean anyway," Mrs. Kowalski said. "The old way's the best way." And she resumed her time-honored habit of boiling sheets on the stove. But the washing machine remained, a strange object of plastic and gleaming glass, proudly on display for when her son came home.

Magda smiled to herself, remembering.

"Can I ask you something?" said Anwen, resting her knitting on her lap.

"Of course."

"Did someone really steal your car? I mean—how did you get a car in the first place?"

"Yes. Someone took it, but it was not really ours. But we did not steal it," Magda said. "Not really. It was in London. We—" She looked at her feet, twisted the cloth in her hands.

"Now, now. Don't worry. I don't need to know," said Anwen. "I think you're an honest girl. Lord knows I wouldn't last three minutes in London. Everything's changed and we've all got to make the best of a bad situation."

"Yes—"

"Anyway, I think I'll have a lie-down for a bit, until Bran and Ivan come back from doing the roof." She rolled up her knitting and put it on the chair. "Make yourself at home."

"Thank you," said Magda.

Home. That would be something.

• • •

"No. It's further up—" Bran held the bottom of an old wooden ladder and Ivan, at the top of it, reached out over the slates of the barn roof. "Just push the slate in where it's slipped down," Bran shouted. The collie sniffed along the wall.

Ivan glanced down with a quizzical look and Bran made a pushing motion with his hand. "Up. Push it up, boyo."

From the house, Callum Gourty strode along in the lee of the drystone wall that bordered the snowy field. He raised a hand at Bran down by the barn, and smiled. *Old codger, got the boy working already.* As he drew nearer, he could smell the sheep. Could hear them rustling and bleating in the barn.

"Got him working already, Bran?"

"No point keeping a dog and barking yourself," Bran said. The collie came over and sniffed at Callum's leg, wagging its tail.

"You need that new pup Huw Thomas has got ready."

"He'll charge me enough, I reckon," said Bran.

"Oh, I don't know. He can't feed a dog he isn't using."

"But what about Mag then?" Mag the collie looked up at the sound of her name. "I can't afford to feed *two* dogs."

"Can't help with that one," Callum said. "But there's no getting round it. You'll need a youngster once the sheep get out on the hill."

"It better be soon too," said Bran. "There's not much feed left."

"You know they dropped hay out on the hill the other night. Up near Huw's place."

"Yes, well it would be a damn sight better if they got the roads clear and the power back on."

"True enough." Callum laughed. "True enough."

Ivan came down the ladder, having successfully wedged the slipped tile back in place.

"Now then," said Bran. "You can have a go at fixing the door, boy." He led the way to the end of the barn, where it was plain to see the old wooden doors were sorely in need of work. There was a wheelbarrow of tools with a stack of planks balanced on top of them. Bran pointed out the loose and broken bits of the door and held up a saw and hammer. Ivan nodded and starting poking about at the rotten wood while Bran and Callum went into the barn and moved about among the sheep.

They were talking in a language Ivan could not understand, and he did not care much, for he was only counting the days. With his own fire and a warm girl.

It could have been worse.

Physical hardship was not much to Ivan. He had always been hungry, or bruised, or a little cold, or too cold, or too hot and never a bed to call his own. The only thing that had been truly his was Anna.

And now there was Magda. With her certainty, and her way of doing things. The strangeness of her country ways. And loving him.

She had surprised him when she said she loved him. She had said it in the bed last night because she did not fear herself.

But one thing Ivan knew about was human weakness. He knew things could never be taken for granted. The darkness always came back.

• • •

Bran looked over his shoulder at all the noise. "Ivan. Steady, boy. Hammer like that and you'll split the damn wood!"

SPRING

And the Spirit of Love leaned so close in the dark that the girl felt its breath on her cheek.

"You cannot build a house of gingerbread," it whispered. "For the summer will turn it to ruin, and love will not care if you are buried in the snow. These mountains won't care. The birds and the wolves will not ask for you. The stones and the rivers will not mind if you are gone."

"*Love?*" cawed Crow from the rafters. "*That old chestnut!*"

And the girl did not cry out, but was silent as ever. For the house, she was certain, was built on foundations of stone. And the summer was yet to come.

28

It was that first day: that first morning with a fuggy haze and un-frosted dew and a throaty pigeon calling from a branch and that old slanty sun rising high enough—just—to bring the smell of things warming and uncoiling within the earth.

It was a day like that.

A haze of woodsmoke sat about the roof of the farm and sig-naled breakfast. Ivan smelled it before he saw it. He had woken early and restless, and was now busy cutting back brambles from the path to the woodshed.

He straightened himself, stretched, and made his way to the back door, his boots damp from the wet grass.

He came into the house and Magda was there cleaning the stove in the dimness of the neat kitchen. The walls were pregnant with the smell of smoke. It got into every bit of clothing. Your hair and your skin even.

But the table was scrubbed clean and the pots laid up on the shelf. There was a sprig of holly in a jar on the windowsill, and the range would soon be as clean as a button. She was busy with these things. He saw it. Like a nesting sparrow.

He did not go to his place at the table, rather he greeted her briefly, then stomped up the worm-eaten stairs to the bedroom.

Magda heard him lifting the floorboard. She had not thought about it for some time. The bundles of passports stuffed under a loose plank. *Gulbekhian.* Her heart beat fast. Ivan came back down.

"What were you doing up there?" she said.

He threw himself roughly into a chair and slapped both his hands down on the scrubbed planks. Arms outstretched. "Look at me. I look like a peasant."

Magda stared across at his dirty hands, cut by brambles and dirt under the fingernails. *Should you tell him now? Are you even sure?* "There is nothing wrong with working in the earth," she said quietly.

He picked up his egg and began to peel the shell.

"Why can you not be happy here?" she went on. "We have the house. No one has come looking for us."

He looked up. "What about your mother, Magda? You don't speak of her anymore."

"Because I don't know where she is."

"It's spring now. We can find Gulbekhian in Liverpool and get back to Krakow, get the money." He put the egg, whole, into his mouth.

"Maybe there is nothing back there," Magda said. "Things are still bad everywhere. It is you who always talks of today. Today is good. Here."

"I promised to deliver the package."

"Oh, so now you don't think that things have changed, that things don't look a little different?"

"What?"

"You said that to me in Krakow. *Can't you see, Magda, things have changed?*"

"It is not what I meant."

"What did you mean? What is wrong with being here?"

"I don't want to live like this, Magda. I don't want to have dirty hands and an aching back and no salt on my food. You really like it that much?"

"We have each other, don't we?" she said. "Why can't we wait a little longer. Until we know more?"

She tried to see something soft in him. Sometimes in the dark of the night she saw something soft in his eyes. When he needed her. But it was not as simple as she had imagined, this *love.* And now here he was prizing up the floorboards and thinking of going to Gulbekhian. After all these months.

Ivan did not look at her softly now. He did not say another word until he had finished his food. "I won't get the money until I go back to Krakow. You know that. It's your money too."

"But you can't know that your bandit friends are still there in Krakow, or even this Gulbekhian in Liverpool? You know nothing of how it might be. Even to go there will be so hard."

Ivan stood up, pushed back the chair. "I thought you were different, Magda." He took the snare from the back of the kitchen door. "I thought you were strong." He slung his bag over his shoulder and left the house without a backward glance.

You must tell him. Tomorrow maybe, she thought. *Today he is just angry.* But she had a terrible feeling, something growing inside her, that it was more than that. A wave of tiredness overtook her. She rearranged their belongings on the shelf: the few books she had taken from the house, the jar of holly twigs and the old coins she had found when digging the patch of earth by the back door. But it would not distract her, so she crept up the stairs and lay down on the bed.

. . .

She woke an hour later with the sound of Ivan feeding sticks into the stove. She swung her legs over the mattress and came downstairs. A handful of wild fennel and a dead hare on the table.

"Are you better now?" she asked, snuggling close by his side and bending her head to his chest with her arms around his waist. "Don't be angry, Ivan. Please." Her finger found a hole in his sweater. "You're always getting holes in everything."

"I've got to skin the hare." He pulled away from her and took his knife from the shelf.

"Well, don't get blood all over the table," she said. "Take it outside."

Ivan carried the hare out onto the grass and rolled up his sleeves. Magda sat heavily on the stone step of the porch and watched him work.

"Why do you want to leave? It isn't so bad here."

He looked up. "I've got a feeling things will be worse if the winter is cold again. And if someone comes asking questions, what will we do?"

Magda thought about the journey in the truck. Everything that had happened. Her hands began to tremble a little, but she

240

hid them in her lap, tried to sound calm. "Maybe your friends in Krakow are not there anymore. What will we do then?"

We? We? The word sat behind Ivan's eyes like a cold, hard stone. *But there was some truth in her words.* The darkness of the loneliness that had followed him like a hungry dog since childhood, it had seeped away a little. He had been happy here in his own way. *You are a real Ukrainian wolf, Ivanchik!* Valentin always said. Valentin did not have earth beneath his fingernails, or porridge in his guts.

Ivan got up and pushed past her. He stuffed the hare into a lidded pot on the kitchen table and stomped back out, pulling down his shirtsleeves. "Gulbekhian will be there in Liverpool."

"Always this *Gulbekhian!*" she snapped.

"Shh—" Ivan tipped his head.

Mrs. Gourty was coming through the apple trees with Alice skipping beside her. Ivan grabbed his jacket and strode past the old woman with the most cursory of nods, and he was over the gate and off down to the stream and into the woods beyond.

"What's wrong with him?" asked Mrs. Gourty.

Magda hauled herself up. "Oh, nothing."

"Mummy's come back!" Alice blurted out, throwing herself around Magda's legs.

"Bethan is *here?*" said Magda.

"Near enough." Mrs. Gourty beamed. "Callum is bringing her up from the Barmouth boat."

"What good news." Magda stroked Alice's head and the little girl beamed up.

"Yes, yes," said Mrs. Gourty. "Anwen's like a headless chicken in there. You must come and help get Alice cleaned up and put the water on the boil for the wash."

"I think the washing will have to wait for another day if Bethan's coming today."

"Can't afford to miss this good weather, Magda," said Mrs. Gourty. "You'll have damp sheets hanging in the barn all week if it rains again. You should have been here when Alice was little and a thousand nappies a day on the line. Poor Anwen. Suppose you'll be thinking of having children yourself one day."

Magda blushed.

"Wouldn't want to be bringing children into the world these days. Mind you, it's different enough when you're young and you just get like a bird wanting to make a nest and lay eggs in it. Can't do anything about that when it happens."

"You sound like my grandmother."

Mrs. Gourty laughed. "No doubt I do. Right, Alice, let's get you ready to see Mummy."

Alice dropped what she was doing and jumped up. "Mummy coming back. Mummy coming back." She pulled on Magda's hand. There was no need to drag the child out of Magda's kitchen today.

They stood for a moment, Mrs. Gourty and Magda, looking out across the orchard. The day had come up bright like its early promise.

"Should be a good crop of apples if you get a bit of sun this summer," Mrs. Gourty said.

And an old crow, sitting in an apple tree, swept out across the orchard at the sound of that noisy child and the sight of that homely back door with women chatting on the step.

Mrs. Gourty pointed after it. "Get your washing done quick, Magda—one crow alone, a sign of foul weather, for sun and good cheer there'll be two crows together—"

"I think the day will be fine," said Magda, smiling. "My grandmother would have told you that was foolish superstition!" And she pulled on her boots and went with Mrs. Gourty and the prancing child up through the orchard.

Yes, everything will be fine. Whatever else happens—spring is on its way. The daughter has come home and tonight you will make a good stew with the hare and Ivan will be happy again.

• • •

They had not seen Callum Gourty so well turned out nor as cleanly shaved as he was when he came up through the still-bare trees with Bethan Mortimer seated beside him on the cart.

Even the pony had been brushed to a shine. With a plait in its tail!

"Mummy!" Alice ran down faster than Anwen could stop her and Callum pulled up the pony and Bethan jumped off and picked the little girl up in her arms and kissed her, and then she came up to the house and there was much greeting and hugging and soon they were seated around Anwen's kitchen table with cups of tea.

• • •

Bethan was an attractive young woman with an unmade-up face and the hint of a laugh about her eyes and mouth. She wore clothes that were old but that had been put together with some care.

243

"The house looks clean," she said, Alice glued to her lap.

"All thanks to Magda," said Anwen.

"It's so good to be home." Bethan relaxed in her chair, suddenly looking tired. Alice snuggled against her, thumb in mouth. "Has Alice been all right?"

"Oh yes, she's been well. Missing you though. But tell us, what's it like in Liverpool?"

"Well, they dropped our wages. Again."

"Again?" said Bran.

"They can treat us how they like, with so many people looking for jobs. But the hotel has been as busy as anything. I pinched some soap for you before I left—"

"Bethan!"

"Oh, come on, Mum. They're making enough out of us already."

"Are you still working with that girl you like?"

"Yes. She's staying on for the summer though."

"Do you think you'll still have a job to go back to?"

"I don't know." Bethan kissed Alice on the head and smelled the child's hair. "I don't know if I'll go back this time."

There was a moment of silence around the table.

"Well, that's the best news we've all heard in a long time," said Anwen. "Isn't it?"

Callum reddened and mumbled in the affirmative.

But Bethan had begun to cry.

Anwen got up and put her arms around her daughter. Said quietly, "It's for the best, love. We don't want you to go away again."

Bran looked down, embarrassed, his hands clasping his mug of tea.

Bethan sniffed and wiped at her red face. "It's getting so bad now. You don't know the half of it. People are talking about all sorts of things that might happen—and if I can't bring back a bit of money, who can?"

"Now come on, love. We'll find a way somehow, won't we, Bran?"

Bran nodded. "It's not the end of the world, Bethan. Just a few bad winters. Let's enjoy today without thinking about such things. Eh?"

"Magda made me snowshoes," said Alice.

"Did she?" Bethan snuffled and tried to smile. "She made you snowshoes? Lucky you."

Then she looked up at all the friendly faces around the table and burst once more into tears.

29

Magda had taken Mrs. Gourty's warning of rain quite seriously after all, so she excused herself and got on with the washing. Her hair was tied back and she was sweating a little with the exertion. For it was a fair bit of work pounding the sheets in the copper tub.

"They're not going to want us about now that *she's* back."

She jumped at the sound of Ivan's voice. Wiped a strand of hair off her forehead with the back of her wet hand. "Ivan. I didn't hear you come in."

"Well, they're not, are they?"

Magda picked up the empty bucket and went to the sink.

Ivan grabbed her arm. "They're not going to want us here, Magda."

She stopped. "You don't know that, Ivan. Think of all the things we do for them. I don't know how they would manage without us."

"Well, I don't want to sit here like a tame pigeon. Working for nothing except turnips."

"How can you say that? They feed us turnips because that's all they've got, and they didn't need to. They could have told the soldiers. Left us out in the snow."

"So we just stay here forever."

"We are very lucky. You didn't hear what Bethan said about the city—"

"Lucky? I don't feel lucky. We can go now on this boat and get back to Poland, make some money. Maybe head east. Make a home somewhere the sun shines, and we won't have to wear ourselves out chopping logs and digging the earth. Look at your hands, Magda. Look at them."

But she didn't. She looked up at his face. "I am happy here, Ivan. With you. It doesn't have to be forever. But for now it's good."

"We came here to find your mother and you don't talk about that much anymore, do you?"

"Don't pretend you came here to help me find her, Ivan. You let me come with you because I had the money."

"You know that's not true," he said. "You know that is not the reason." He pulled her close, but she was stiff in his arms. "I liked you the first time I saw you sweating away in the snow on the mountain. Never looking back. Remember? You didn't look back then."

She set her face in defiance. "It's not me looking back, Ivan. It's you."

And she pushed past him and went to the pump for more water.

Her hands shaking.

• • •

That afternoon, when the others returned, Magda sat at the table and listened with half her heart to Bethan's stories of the city. And when it was time enough she said goodnight to them all, and at last she made her way down the darkened corridor to her own kitchen.

247

It was very late by the time Ivan returned. Quietly through the back door. Hanging his bag on the hook.

He ate the stew.

Magda watched him with her still-shaking hands in her lap.

But he did not talk about Gulbekhian and going back.

And when they were in the darkness of their bed he was very soft and gentle with her and afterward he lay for a long time looking at the side of her face in the candlelight.

Havemercy. He remembered her calling out in the forest. And how he had thought of helping her. Then finding her in Krakow. He had not needed her. Not even her money. It was only now that it came to him, came to him that things were not so simple within his heart: that, though she was drawn to him, he too was drawn to her.

"You'll always settle down and make a nest, won't you," he said fondly. "Wherever you land. Even if it's just a couple of twigs in a bare tree."

Magda turned her head, her hair rustling on the pillow. "Why do you say that?"

He closed his eyes and breathed in the smell of her.

"I love you, Magda," he said.

It was the first time.

So easy it was for the demons to grow silent.

He loves you. And you love him. And everything will be all right.

And without a ripple now disturbing the pool, Magda fell asleep with her head on his shoulder at last.

But the new day would come.

It was barely light outside.

Paleness rimming about the hills.

A blackbird—*chee chee cheeee cheeee chee*—dipped past the window and woke Magda from her sleep.

She sat up in the bed. Queasy in her stomach.

Instinctively she felt for Ivan beside her.

The sheet was cold.

He has probably gone out to fetch wood.

She got up and pulled a blanket about her, stepped down the stairs, hand against the wall in the dimness.

The kitchen was empty. The faint lingering of warmth in the burnt-down stove. Table clean and tidied from the night before. The remains of last night's stew in the pot.

Smiling, she went to the door and unlatched it. Stood out on the damp step with the first birds singing.

"Ivan?" she called.

It had rained in the night. The long grass was wet with it.

"Ivan?"

The birds seemed so loud. The tiny leaves on the hawthorn coming now so fresh and green, sprays of white mayflowers among the matted branches and the spiders' webs glistening in the dew of the hedge.

There was no sign of him.

She went back inside, pulled the door, and looked behind it.

His bag was not there.

She tapped with her hand. His knife—gone from the shelf.

Maybe he has gone out for a hare?

But her heart beat like a drum as she hurried back up the stairs and knelt down on her knees by the bed, prizing frantically at the floorboard.

The board came away easily enough.

She rummaged with her hand. Maybe they were pushed further underneath.

But they were not.

The bundle of passports was gone.

And yet the roll of money. The last of the money for Bogdan Stopko's pony. She counted the notes. Two hundred and forty zloty. He had halved it

It came to her in that instant.

She fell forward, bent over with her long hair pooling on the dark floorboards, head in her hands, thumbs pressing stars into her screwed-up eyes.

It came from the very depths of her quaking guts, without a bend in the river or any impediment, a pool that welled up from her simple heart and burst from behind her eyes and poured from her mouth in a cry that filled her head and her body and every single part of her.

Ivan had gone.

And she knew, because he had not told her, because he had crept away like a thief in the night leaving half the money, that he was not coming back.

She dragged herself up from the floor and leaned against the wall.

I love you, Magda.

Why why why?

And she saw herself. And not for the first time. A foolish country girl with hair smeared across her wet face.

This was the new day and what it had brought.

You had not told him, you had not told him.

And the tears came again and she crawled onto the bed.

And that is how Anwen found her, with the swollen-uddered cows calling out by the gate:

"Magda—the milking. It's seven already!"

SUMMER

Then the night grew dark as soot.

And words that Crow had spoken rang like Clappers in Bells.

"*If you but cry out once, my misery will be doubled.*"

And the Spirit of Faith sang from the Chimney and circled her head like a shadow of bats. It beat about her face and tangled in her hair and hung from the mantel with tiny sharp claws.

"Faith!" cawed Crow from its lofty perch. "Faith always sings in the dark."

And still the girl was silent. Alone on that wide, wide bed as the flames in the fire grew low.

30

But the hands of the clock—the old long-case clock in the stone-flagged hallway at Rathged Farm—would not stop their working round: second by second, minute by minute, hour by hour, day by day.

The sun crept up, unveiled by those clouds that had swollen the stream and wet the slates on every roof for seven whole days.

Behind the fluttering, full-leafed apple trees below her window, Magda's sleep had been restless as usual.

She had woken early, enjoying, for that brief moment of deliverance, the light on the sill and the promise of a new day. But like every waking moment of calm, all her certainty had crumpled in a second like a castle of dust.

The sheet still bare beside her.

Dressing slowly, she went to the window and put her sad head against the pane.

Did she expect to see him down there, looking up at her window? Even now? Had she really waited so long?

• • •

She went out to the waiting cows in the milking shed. Their warm smell and prodding noses were her morning comfort now. When the urn was full of milk, she lugged it to the dairy, lifting the heavy latch with one hand and pushing her way inside with her elbow.

The room was cool and quiet with that sweet sour smell from the scrubbed benches. The bowls sat clean and washed from the day before.

She took out last night's milk and placed the new urn into the bucket of cold spring water and covered it with a cloth for the cream to rise.

The curd cheese that had been hanging in muslin bags was strained, and Magda filled clean bowls with it, sealing the tops with boiled cloth and wooden lids. She tied each bowl with string to make a handle on the top and layered them in sturdy boxes. The curd cheese always sold, and the hard cheese, the ones she could spare, fetched enough money to buy salt.

She had made twelve pairs of snowshoes from the hazel rods Bran cut for her, and they were tied in bundles by the door.

"You do that cleverly enough," Bran had said. "But people forget the snow when the sun's shining. No one will buy them."

"Yes they will," Magda told him. "You'll see."

But she hadn't really cared whether they would or not. The main thing was to keep busy. If that meant blistered palms from bending sticks, or sore feet from standing over the cheese, or aching arms from sweeping the kitchen floor, or fingers pricked from darning Alice's socks—it was all one to her.

She followed the day with these chores, chasing the hands of the clock until bedtime came around and sleep gave her some peace from thoughts of Ivan.

• • •

The crunch of wheels in the yard signaled Callum's arrival. He had come up to the house with the stocky pony, Mill Boy, hitched to the cart.

Magda came out to greet him, folding her apron in her hands. She looked over the rail at his bundles of sheepskins and jars of honey. "I'll bring the cheese out," she said. "I've packed it in boxes. Where's your mother? Isn't she coming too?"

"She's not feeling too well, hasn't got over her cold yet."

"I think I'll go with you then," said Magda. "I can give you a hand and the change of scenery would be good."

"What about Bethan?" said Callum, looking disappointed.

"I'll run in and ask her." Magda smiled. "I'm sure Alice would enjoy the ride."

• • •

And so it was that Callum Gourty went to market with two young women and an excited little girl sitting up beside him on the seat. He slapped the reins on the pony's back and they jolted off down the drive, out between the old stone gateposts of Rathged Farm and onto the overgrown lane that led down to Dolgellau.

The wheels rumbled and creaked over the narrow roads where mossy grass now clung to the tarmac and dandelions found purchase in a thousand cracks. And happy enough was Callum Gourty with Bethan Mortimer swaying beside him.

"It's been a good summer," Bethan said. "Maybe we'll have an easy winter of it this year. It can't go on getting colder and colder, can it? Things will get back to normal—surely."

Magda pulled Alice up onto her lap and held her little hands, clapped them gently together.

"Clap, clap, little hands,
Babula is still in bed,
Babula will give us milk;
While dya-dya bakes a gingerbread."

"More, more!" Alice chortled. "More."

The cart rolled along and everyone fell silent, even Alice. There was a kind of soporific rhythm to it, the tail of the pony swishing now and then, the nodding of its head. The sound of metal rims on the grassy road.

"Look! It's Huw and Geraint," Bethan said.

Callum looked out across the fields and saw the old man and his son shepherding a large flock of sheep down the hill.

He stopped the cart by a gap in the hedge and waved. "Hulloooo!"

Geraint cantered over the meadow to the cut in the road and came clattering up, his pony sweaty-necked and breathing hard.

"Hello there." Geraint was awkward in his eighteen-year-old body. A soft downy sprouting of dark hairs creeping over his face. A lock of thick black hair hung over his forehead. He pushed it back, reddening slightly.

"Where are you lot off to then, like?"

Callum thumbed back at the boxes loaded onto the cart. "Dolgellau market."

"I can see you've brought a fishing rod—"

"That too." Callum smiled. "Might go down to Bontwerduu Pool if I get time. Where are you taking the sheep?"

"Barmouth. Slaughtering the lot of them."

"Slaughtering them. All?"

"Dad's decided to farm deer now. Got a grant to put a fence up and everything."

"A grant?" Callum sounded surprised.

"Went up to Manchester and arranged it with DEFRA," said Geraint proudly. "It's the food shortages. They give you a grant and buy everything you produce. We'll have to get papers and special licenses and all that."

"Why not stick with the sheep?"

"We've been lambing in the snow for the last six years. Dad's tired of it. We'll end up with the same money for the deer and less work of it."

"Looks like he needs you," said Bethan, pointing across the field.

Geraint turned in the saddle, one hand on the pony's rump. His father was waving angrily from the hillside, the flock parting.

"Coc!" Geraint pulled the pony's head up from the grassy verge. "Better get back before he loses his rag proper like." And they all laughed as he kicked the unfortunate beast up the bank and back across the field toward his irate father.

• • •

Down in the valley, rising and falling with the tides that swept up from the Barmouth estuary, was the wide-banked River Mawddach, glinting here and there between the stands of low trees. And from the newly built jetty in Barmouth harbor, the Liverpool boat unloaded its passengers into long, sturdy dinghies that ferried punters upriver to the Dolgellau market.

Callum pulled up on the old stone bridge outside the village.

"Look at that."

Early as it was, there were already people carrying boxes from the riverbank with baskets and bags and folded trestles and dinghy men shouting and helping women off.

"When we've sold everything, I need to go to the Stag."

"What is the Stag?" asked Magda.

"It's the pub," said Bethan. "Callum always gets a barrel of beer from Vince the landlord."

• • •

Vince Price heard the rumbling of cartwheels. He looked out from a small, grimy window in the storeroom of the Stag as a horse and cart passed by on the street outside. He recognized Callum Gourty. Couple of pretty girls up back too.

Vince rubbed the side of his beaky nose. Turned to the tired-looking man with thick reddish hair seated at the table.

"Well, so what are you going to do then?"

"Sit tight, I reckon," said the man.

"You know they're looking for you, Robin."

"Reckon they are."

A grubby little child played with a piece of wood and an old snooker ball under the table.

"And?"

"Reckon I'll keep low. Keep working away."

"I'm risking a lot for you, you know that?"

"I know."

"I've spoken to Mr. Ip about the ink. He'll be in here later too. I asked him to bring some. But it isn't going to come cheap."

The man nodded. "You know where to find me." He got up, his tall, lean form giantlike next to Vince. The child crawled out from under the table without needing to be told, and Vince opened the door that led out to the dank yard above the cellar where a small pony was waiting.

"You all right up there? Without Sarah?" he said, helping the child onto the pony behind the man.

"We get by." And without too many other words the tall red-haired man kicked the pony on and went up through the narrow lanes that led out behind the houses to the dark of the Coed-y-Brenin forest, a dark shelter on the distant hills beyond.

• • •

Back in the pub there was a loud banging on the door. The Liverpool slaughter-men wanting to get on the grog before the day had started. Big, hard men from the city, come up for cutting throats in the slaughter sheds by the river.

"Oy! Open up!" they shouted.

"Hold your bleedin' horses!" Vince stumped toward the old heavy door and pulled back the bolts. "Patience's bleedin' virtue, mate."

Two men with drawn faces stumbled across the step and smirked. "Where's the beer, man. I'm parched."

"Yeah, yeah." Vince went back behind the high-topped bar and tapped a couple of pints from the barrel on the wide shelf. "Five quid."

"I'm not paying that for weak fockin' ale, man."

"Well, that's all you *fockin'* getting," said Vince, banging the glass down on the counter. "Money—"

Everyone knew that Cockney Vince was as tough as a badger so the slaughter-men handed over their cash and went to drink in silence on the old wooden pew by the unlit fire.

Vince cleaned glasses and kept his watchful eyes on them. He'd seen it all before, few hours of fresh air and lads from the city, on God knows what business, always sucked like water in a drain toward the dark corners of the grog house. The slaughter-men at least had some excuse for watering the cold light of day. And money was money.

Coming out on the boat was a bit of a holiday for him and Irene—good to come back to the old place and air out the rooms for a month or two. Irene, the lazy slattern, still in bed. He went to the doorway marked PRIVATE and hollered up the stairs. "Oy, Irene, get yer lazy arse out of bed. We've got customers."

• • •

Callum led the way, stooping his tall frame under the low door of the pub. The room was dingy and smoke-filled. A menacing group of slaughter-men sauntered by the bar with greedy eyes and bloodstained fingernails, clasping glasses of Vince's dark brown ale.

They turned and stared at Magda and Bethan. One of the men raised his glass. "Come over here, lass."

Callum glared. "You two sit down with Alice, out of their way."

"What's your problem, mate?" one of the slaughter-men shouted over. "You got enough women there to spare one."

"Do you think this is a good idea, Callum?" said Bethan, pulling Alice onto her lap as they squashed at a table.

"Ignore them. I'll go and see about the beer."

Callum leaned over the counter. Vince was busy tapping pints and a flustered Irene was taking money.

"Callum!" she exclaimed. "Good to see you. Now then, what'll you have?"

"I'd like to get a barrel of beer."

One of the slaughter-men banged his empty glass on the counter. "Another ale!"

"You wait your turn, lad. Vince!" She turned to her husband. "Callum Gourty's here."

Vince swiveled around, still pulling a pint under the barrel. "Callum! Ain't seen you in a while. Saw you go by loaded to the eaves with stuff. Sell it all?"

"Yes," Callum shouted. "Sold the lot." He waved a thick wad of cash over the bar with a grin and peeled off a stack of notes. "Enough for a barrel this autumn."

"Sure, I'll have one for you by Monday. I might bring it up. Just the one?"

"One's enough for me."

"See you've got the prettiest girls in town," said Irene.

"I'm not waitin' all day, woman." The slaughter-man barged in, slamming his empty glass down. Irene scowled, but went to fill it, not wanting the trouble. "So, everything well up at Rathged?" she said, ignoring the uncouth slurping at her shoulder. "Still got the ponies?"

"Yes. We're fine. We'll be well stocked this winter. Are you and Vince staying in Liverpool over winter again?"

"Yes, and we're buying a place up in Manchester. The King Will, down on the canal. Should be good business. Hope we can come out next summer though. I don't like it in town."

"No, me neither," said Callum. "See you on Monday then."

• • •

The slaughter-man at the bar watched Callum leaving with his women. He had listened well, and noted the fat roll of money in his pocket. Rathged Farm. Ponies. He turned back to his friends, finished the dregs in his glass, and kept his own counsel. For now.

31

"Bontwerduu Pool. I'm going to see if I can catch a fish. The rain will have swollen the river, should be easy."

Callum unhitched the pony and hobbled it above the bank. It stuck its nose down and began tearing at the grass.

They walked along the path and clambered down through the bushes and rocks toward the sound of the water.

Bethan and Magda lay down in the shade of a tree and Alice poked around on the bank, watching ants and throwing pebbles into the water.

Rolling up his trousers, Callum waded through the shallows with the fishing rod in his hand.

It wasn't long before his cork bobbed down and the line cut a slice through the water. "Got you!" He flicked the end of his rod up and fought the thrashing fish to the water's edge.

He looked over to the others. "Alice! Don't go too far. Don't go further than we can see you." There was a flash of a tail in the pool and Callum concentrated his efforts once more. And soon there were three shiny trout on the bank.

• • •

"Mummy!" Alice slipped down the bank. "Mummy! Pony gone!"

Bethan sat up. "Callum—"

Callum waded over and threw his rod down. "What?"

"Pony gone," Alice said.

They scrambled up the bank and raced along the path to the road.

The cart was there, traces and yoke hanging over the shafts as they had been left. But the pony was not.

Callum leaned down and retrieved the leather hobble that had been cast aside onto the grass.

"It's been cut. Someone has stolen Mill Boy."

"What are we going to do?"

There was a clopping on the lane and from around the bend Geraint and his father, Huw, came trotting down the road on their tired horses with their sheepdog close at heel, his tongue lolling out with the run.

"You lot look like you've seen a ghost," Huw Thomas said, pulling up his horse and seating himself back in the saddle.

"Some bastard's stolen the pony," said Callum. "Did you see anyone on the road?"

"Not a thing, Gourty." In an instant, Huw was all seriousness. "But Geraint can get the women back to Dolgellau and you can ride down the Barmouth road with me. Right—Geraint lad, you hear me, get those women and that cart up to the Stag and no arsing around."

He leaned down and pulled Callum up onto his own pony, then kicked it on in the direction of Dolgellau with Callum bouncing, ungainly, behind the saddle.

Geraint was shy to be left alone with the women, and so he

busied himself energetically with unsaddling his horse and getting it between the empty shafts of Callum Gourty's cart.

"Now don't you cry, Alice. Here, have an apple." Geraint took a small red apple from his pocket. The pony pricked its ears, but Geraint pushed its nose away and gave the apple to Alice, sitting up on the seat. She stopped her snuffling and took it in her hand.

"Come, boy," said Geraint, and he led the pony on and up the road with the dog zig-zagging across their path, snuffling about the hedgerows and verges as it went.

• • •

Back in Dolgellau at last, the girls sat and waited in the empty pub. When Irene had finished cleaning, she came over and sat down on the bench beside them.

"I reckon it'll 'ave been one of those slaughter-men. They're a rough bunch and no morals either."

Bethan was very glum. "It's a bad loss for Callum. For all of us, I suppose."

"I know, love. I bet it is. But Huw will help. He's not as hard as he looks when there's the taste of being a hero in the air. I remember once when my car broke down, years ago up near his place when we were still living out here. He had his tractor towing it back to the village in no time."

"Mum will be wondering where we are by now," Bethan said.

The men came ducking in under the open door.

"No. Nothing," said Huw. "We can't do a thing more. It'll be dusk soon."

Callum sat, a frown between his eyes.

The pony was gone and nowhere to be seen. Not on the Barmouth trail nor in any direction they could make out, even though they had ridden Huw's tired horse as hard and as far as they reasonably could.

"Now then, don't you worry, ladies," said Huw, looking at the downcast faces. "Geraint will get the cart back and you on it. And we ought to leave soon. Don't want to be out in the dark, Gourty. Not with thieving townies around."

"Are your horses fit enough for it?" said Callum.

"They may be tired," said Huw, "and us as well, but if you can't help a neighbor in need and the women there and the kiddy too . . . No, the ponies can rest well enough when they get home. Now, Geraint, you get these people home and then straight back."

It was a very sorry end to an otherwise successful day, and they all sat silent on the journey home that seemed thrice as long as it had on the way down, with dark thoughts creeping in the mossy dusk and all of them wondering what sort of people there were abroad.

"You know it's the last day of summer," said Bethan, looking out across the fields at the dropping sun. "I just remembered."

It was indeed.

AUTUMN

It was plain to see. In the cold light of day. That the walls of Crow's Hall were only bare branches, and the girl's bed was just a mossy bank, with the ceiling vaulted by trees and the sky her roof.

Yet still she would not cry out.

For the Spirit of Hope had come scratching at the bank, and it curled at her back in the cold of the dawn.

"Hope! That penniless fool?" cawed Crow, pulling worms in the field.

But she listened not to Crow.

32

It was that hastening time at the end of the year when leaves fall from the trees and threads of geese take to the sky.

Today it is a sky of palest blue. So pale it is almost gray. And the morning air is so damp with hovering mists that you can smell it.

Everyone at Rathged was tired as old horses with all the summer's dragging of scythes, and bundling of hay and thrashing of oats.

Magda went down to light the stove. There was a footfall on the step. She switched her gaze to the door with a flurrying heart.

But it was only Bethan.

"Magda? You up? Just want to come and sit in your calm for a minute if that's all right."

"You are awake very early, Bethan."

"So are you. Dad's going to Barmouth tomorrow—do you need anything?"

"Just soap and some more thread."

"I'll tell him."

"I am going to look for mushrooms," Magda said. "I think it's the last day for it. Will you eat some breakfast with me before I go out?"

She cut some cheese and took out a stool for Bethan and sat

with her in the open back door, the fire beginning to crack and the logs shifting in the stove at their backs.

There was a chill to the air already.

Bethan leaned over, resting her forearms on her thighs. She wiggled her toes in her boots, staring down at them, caked with dirt as they were.

"I used to be really into shoes," she said. "You know. Before."

Magda smiled.

"What about you, Magda? Don't you wish it would all just—go away?"

"I thank God that I found this place."

"God? You actually think he exists? Up there in the sky. Sort of sitting on a cloud or something."

Magda laughed. "Well, I have to believe in something."

"Magda, you're so—I don't know."

"What?"

"Never mind." Bethan sat up straight. "If you went back to Poland, do you think you'd find him again?"

Magda turned to her friend. "Even if I did, Bethan, Ivan did not want me."

"You don't know what he was thinking. Maybe he will come back."

They were silent for a while, looking out under the trees. "You'll be lonely here, won't you?" Bethan said quietly.

"Maybe." A small cloud passed under the hazy sun. And a soft dimness fell across the orchard.

"Do you think we'll be all right this winter? You know for food and stuff—"

Magda looked back under the trees. "We'll get hungry just like the birds. But we won't starve if we're careful. It has been a good summer. Maybe the winter will not be so hard."

"Callum says it's the calm before the storm."

Magda laughed. "He is not a man filled with lightness."

"Oh, I don't know. He has his moments." Bethan paused. "If it hadn't been for you helping with the dairy and all the other things, I don't know what Mum and Dad would have done. Somehow you manage to keep everything in order. You've always got clean clothes and a tidy place—you're not worried about—you know? When it comes?"

Magda looked away. "I don't want to worry about things that haven't happened."

"Do you think you will go back to Poland? Really—"

"Look at me, Bethan. Do you think I'll be going anywhere soon?" Magda got up like a full stop. Stood, hands over her rounded belly, looking out under the trees. "We must find boxes for storing the apples. It's a good crop. But they will rot if we don't store them well. And the mice. If it is dry tomorrow, we must start picking. And then we can make vinegar and start the bottling. I'm going to take Mrs. Gourty a tea later. You know she is not well."

"I heard," said Bethan.

"Maybe you want to come too? You should see Callum's barn stacked high with logs and hay. He works hard. He is going to take some ponies to Barmouth soon. He has sold them to the man who runs the boat from Liverpool."

"You'd think he'd be a bit lonely with only his mum up there."

"You know he likes you."

"Who? Callum?"

"Yes, of course."

"Really?"

"He won't spill out his heart without you tipping the jug a bit. Good men don't grow in every hedgerow."

Bethan laughed.

Magda gave her a look.

"All right. I'll walk up there later. Is that good enough?"

Magda touched her on the arm. "Don't forget to tell your father about getting the thread and soap."

"You and your soap."

"Don't forget."

"I won't, Magda. I couldn't bear the nagging."

• • •

The woods were quite beautiful. It was cold and bright and the last leaves still drifted down between the damp gray trees.

Magda stepped from the path and began to climb the bank, poking with a stick at the leaf litter.

There! She bent down and cupped her fingers under the fat, round cap of *Boletus edulis,* with its nut-brown head and spongy gills. She poked about in the leaf litter again and found another. She cut the stem with a short knife and, pushing off a slug, she placed it among the bracken laid in her basket.

The basket grew heavier as she ambled through the forest with her eyes to the ground. She was briefly content in her distraction, for by looking for the one thing she could find she might perhaps forget the thing she had lost.

The hours passed almost pleasantly so: birds rising and falling to the forest floor as she passed, and the crisp autumn haze lifting through the trees as she scrambled over damp gray rocks and twisted tree roots. She could almost feel that Babula might be ahead of her, under the broad trees of the forest back home. "Where you find one, Magda, you will find others."

Oh, there are so many. You should have brought another hamper, foolish girl!

She sat down, leaned her back against a tree, and rearranged the precious hoard teetering in her overfull basket. She closed her eyes and tried to push the thoughts of Ivan away.

She woke with a bumblebee buzzing past, clumsy and cold, making the most of the last of the year before it folded its wings and crawled into the earth for the winter. It was time for her to get back home too. She got up, ready to make her way down the slope.

But from the corner of her eye she caught a movement through the trees. She almost shouted out, thinking it was Callum Gourty, for it was definitely a man leading a pony, parallel to her on the slope some two hundred feet away.

But she realized in an instant it was not Callum Gourty at all. The figure was taller than him and, on the pony's back, a child. Instinctively, she dropped down behind a tree.

The man had not seen her and trudged laboriously up the

slope, the rein looped behind him, his figure wavering behind the tree trunks until it could be seen no more.

Magda did not know of anyone who lived nearby. Surely they would have heard of someone living so close as this.

She sat crouching for some time, afraid. But the figure had disappeared on the slope above her.

She made her way down the bank as fast as she could go. Bad thoughts that she was not alone in the forest snapped like wolves at her hurrying feet.

When she came to the stream, she followed the gushing water to a fallen trunk that made a crossing, and soon she was out onto the long grass of the meadows, and up on the other side of the dell.

Above a bluff of craggy gray rock, she could see the Gourtys' place, several ponies with noses to the ground, grazing on the gray-green hill above the farm. Their stocky shapes moved slowly, tails swishing, as they nibbled at the short grass there.

Magda held the basket firm and made her way up toward the house, glancing back at the forest on the hill behind her now and then, pleased to come to the wide wooden gate and the smell of hay and pony. She crossed the cobbled yard to the door of the farmhouse with the comforting smell of woodsmoke in the air, came into the porch and knocked on the door.

"It's me," she called out. "Magda."

The door opened and Callum stood in the entrance, as if he had been making his way outside even as she raised her hand to knock.

"Magda. Come in, come in."

He prodded about in her basket and she held it out. "You've got a nose for it. I can never find a thing, and then you just point down and there they are."

Magda beamed, but hid her pride a little. "I've come to see your mother—"

"Well, she'll be pleased to see you. She hasn't come down yet, so why don't you just go up?"

"I saw someone in the woods," said Magda. She pointed back across the fields. "Over there. A man with a pony, and a child. I'm sure of it."

Callum looked over at the bank of trees. "Oh, aye."

"You don't sound very surprised."

"Not really."

"But who can it be? There's no one else living near here, is there?"

Magda saw on the table several hareskins laid out. Callum followed her gaze. She looked up at him.

"It wasn't a stranger, Magda," he said. "His name is Robin Blake. He gives me skins in return for salt."

"The child on the pony? Is it his?"

"Yes."

"And there is a woman?"

"No. Not anymore."

"How does he look after a child on his own?"

Callum laughed. "He can look after his child all right. The boy's clean enough and fed enough, but maybe it's a funny thing being stuck up in these hills with just Robin for company."

"How do you know him?"

"He bought a pony off me about six years ago. That's how we first met."

"Where does he live?"

"Never you mind, Magda Krol! But I'll tell you this, Robin's likable enough and, even if he doesn't say much, when he does it's worth hearing. But he likes to keep himself to himself pretty much."

Magda put her basket on the table and looked more closely at the furs. "They are well cured. He made them like this himself?"

"Reckon so. Hare mostly."

Magda put her fingers into the softness of them. "They would make some good winter clothes. For the baby."

"Yes. I reckon they would. I was going to take them to Barmouth, but I'll give them to you instead. For a cheese or two, perhaps?"

"Would you? I would like that very much."

"Fair enough, take them when you go. Well, I better get on with the pony now, but Mum will be pleased to see you."

"I'll come and watch after I've seen her."

"Right enough." Callum pulled on his boots at the door and Magda lifted a kettle of water onto the stove and drew a small paper packet of seeds from her pocket.

"What are they?"

"Poppy seeds."

"You're a proper witch, aren't you, Magda?"

"Witch?"

But Callum Gourty just smiled at her, lifted a bridle from the hook in the porch, and stomped out into the yard.

While the tea steeped in the pot, Magda looked again at the hare-skins. There were ten of them, enough for a small jacket and trousers. She thought about the strange man and his lonely child disappearing under the trees.

Her hand lingered, fingers deep in the soft fur. The world was still turning, away out there, away beyond these fields and hills; even in these dark times things did not just disappear. There was still a world out there and Ivan was walking in it somewhere. Mama was out there too. Babula's cottage was still sitting under the hill in Morochov.

What are you doing here? In this strange place with strange people. You have settled down like a cuckoo on a nest.

She felt a movement inside her.

But you cannot go now. Next spring. If things are easier, then you can go to Liverpool on the boat.

Maybe there would be a way back. She still had the remaining zloty tucked under the floorboards.

The tea was ready and she held the warm pot and climbed the stairs to Mrs. Gourty's bedroom, pushing gently at the door. "Mrs. Gourty, it's Magda—"

. . .

Callum was at the end of the barn riding the sweaty pony around in a circle. He turned at Magda's shouts.

"Callum! Come quick. Your mother!"

Callum leapt up the stairs, his heavy boots clomping two steps at a time. Mrs. Gourty was breathing hard, her chest straining. Her eyes were closed and her face was pale.

"What's wrong with her, Magda?"

"I don't know, but she can hardly breathe. Feel her forehead. It's really hot. Can you get her to a doctor? Is there one in Barmouth?"

"Not now. They only come once a week. But the boat's coming tomorrow—Mum, it's all right," Callum said. "There's a boat going to Liverpool in the morning. I didn't think, Magda. She didn't come down this morning, but I didn't think—"

Magda put her hand on his arm. "It's not your fault. But you must take her to a doctor. It's the only thing you can do for her."

"If I go to Liverpool, I won't be back for a week at least. The boat only comes once a week. Someone has to look after the ponies."

"Don't worry. I can take care of that. You must get her ready."

Together they hitched a pony to the light trap in a hasty panic of fingers and buckles. Magda bundled blankets from the bedroom and Callum lifted his mother into his arms and labored down the narrow stairs. They propped her gently in the back of the cart and made her as comfortable as possible. The old lady could barely talk, but her fingers gripped hard on Magda's hand.

"Don't worry, Mrs. Gourty," Magda said. "It will be all right."

Down below them a figure was climbing the fence on the low field.

"It's Bethan." Magda waved her arms frantically. Bethan hurried up the slope toward the house.

"What?" Bethan said, breathless, coming across the yard. "What's wrong?"

. . .

Magda burst through the back door of Rathged Farm.

"What is it?" said Anwen.

"It's Mrs. Gourty. She's ill—Callum has taken her to Barmouth for the Liverpool boat. Bethan's gone with them."

"Bethan?"

The young collie pup ran circles at Magda's feet.

"I said I'd look after the ponies," said Magda. "Alice can come up there with me until Bethan gets back."

"Do you think Mrs. Gourty will be all right?" said Bran.

Magda pushed the pup away from her. "I have a bad feeling about it."

33

It was strange to be alone in Callum Gourty's house. Strange with new smells and new sounds and not knowing really where the plates lay or the pots sat and feeling thief-like, eating the things from his larder and pulling the blankets over her in a strange bed that night. She felt better when Alice came creeping under the covers.

"Magda, look," said Alice, wriggling free from under her arm and sticking her head up over the blanket. "Look! Snowing!"

"Snow?"

"Yes. Look!"

Magda sat up on her elbows. And, yes, snowflakes were fluttering against the glass in the eddies of a wind.

Already? It's barely November.

Alice slipped out from beneath the blankets and padded across the floorboards. She stood on her toes and pressed her nose against the glass. "I can see it on the fields."

"Well, come back into bed then. It won't go away before the morning."

Reluctantly, with a lingering glance at the world outside, Alice came back into the bed and snuggled close. "It's winter now, isn't it?" she said.

"Yes, Alice, I suppose it is."

. . .

Magda woke. It was dark. But the horses were making a commotion in the field. Alice was still asleep and breathing heavy. Very quietly, Magda pulled back the covers and dropped her legs over the side of the bed. The springs creaked, but the child did not stir.

She pulled on her clothes and went to the window. The fields were already white, with grasses poking blades up through the thin snow.

Something moved behind the barn.

Her heart beat fast.

Who could it be? The others? Come to get the ponies in because of the weather?

No. It was a man. Two men.

She pulled back from the window. "Alice," she whispered urgently. "Alice, wake up."

Alice half opened her eyes and turned over and went back to sleep.

"Alice." She shook her gently.

"Is it morning?"

"No. You have to be very quiet, Alice."

"Why?"

"Here, put these on." She dressed the child with fumbling fingers. Outside, the horses whinnied from the field again.

"Why we getting up? It's dark."

"Alice, you're going to have to be very good and do everything I tell you and not make any noise. It's a special game. Do you understand?"

"But why?"

"If you do it very well, I will make you a cake and you can play in the dairy whenever you like."

"A cake!"

"Yes, but remember! Shh!" Magda put her finger over Alice's mouth. The little girl nodded and Magda tied the laces on her shoes.

In the corner of the room was a cupboard. Magda took a large sheepskin coat and wrapped it around the child. "You have to sit in this cupboard, Alice, sit in here and keep as still as a mouse. Whatever you hear and whatever happens. Don't open your mouth or make a move." She leaned down and kissed Alice on the head and stroked her hair.

She could see the whites of the girl's eyes so wide.

"Don't worry, Alice." She closed the cupboard door, wedging it shut with a pair of shoes. With her heart banging in her chest, she came down the creaky stairs.

The smell of the kitchen rose up to greet her. And she stepped onto the flagstones, closed the stair door behind her, turned the lock, and put the key in her pocket.

She waited. Listening. Afraid.

Why did you bring the child here?

But it was too late for that. She stepped to the kitchen window and looked out. The yard was still. There was only the young stallion in the stable. She could just make out his head over the stable door, ears pointed toward the noisy mares in the field.

Maybe just sit tight. If they are thieves, they will only take the ponies.

But the ponies. Callum's ponies.

You can get over to Rathged and fetch the others. Alice is safe. The worst that can happen is that she is afraid. No harm will come to her. Not if you are quick.

She unbolted the front door and lifted the latch. Very slowly, she pushed it open and came out. With one hand she lifted the bridle from its peg in the porch. Closed the door quietly behind her.

The young pony whinnied from across the yard.

She stood still. Listened again.

Voices carried faint in the wind from the top field.

Quickly she stepped across the yard and into the stall. The pony stomped back, snorting. "Be good for me, boy, be good now." She ran her hands over his neck and he stamped his feet and tried to nip her. She brought the bridle over his head, pushing the bit into his soft mouth, pulling the leather over his springy ears.

"Good boy." She lifted the reins over his head and led him quietly from the stable. The darkness calmed him; he was not used to being taken out in the dark.

"Now then, you must promise not to kick." She pulled out a bale and climbed up on it. Grasped the pony's mane and hauled her heavy body onto his warm back.

Magda felt his chomping and pulling as he sidestepped out under the barn door and into the snowy yard. She turned him up toward the track that led behind the house. And when they had come halfway down the edge of the wood, she stopped in the shelter of the dark trees and saw the shadowy figures leading Callum Gourty's ponies in a long string out through the gate toward the Dolgellau road and she kicked the beast on and he flung his head and went faster than it was almost possible for her to bear in her condition and they bore away into the dark of the woods toward Rathged.

34

The new collie pup lay out in the snow behind the back door.

Its head some way from its body.

It was dark, of course, and Magda could not see the redness of the blood. But she could see there was blood—seeping black on the thin snow.

Her breaths that were already so close and short jumped closer up under her ribs and her hand leapt up to her mouth and she let out a cry.

She had almost known when she led the pony into the yard and tied it with hasty, frozen fingers and seen that the store sheds and buildings were all flung open, one chicken sitting flustered on the open stable door in the nighttime. She had known then that something was wrong.

She remembered now the strange marks on the snow along the road and up the drive and mushy in the front although she had ridden over them without thinking somehow.

Tire marks.

But there was no vehicle here now.

The back door was open.

She came into the still-warm kitchen.

God in heaven have mercy. Her hand once more to her mouth.

The table had been shunted across the room and broken glass crunched underfoot.

"Mag?" She called it out quietly. But the old black collie was nowhere to be seen.

With shaking hands, she took a fallen candle off the counter, tapped with her fingers along the shelf, and found the matches.

When she had lit it, she wished she had not.

From the open door to the hallway was a pair of feet. And legs.

Bran. Felled like an oak.

She knelt down beside his prone body. His head was cold against the stone flags. Blood at the mouth. His eyes were open and she closed them.

She stepped over him with her arm to her face and her swollen body doubled, and hauled herself along the passage and into the other room.

It cannot be.

Slumped against the wall, her clothes torn, legs askew, head fallen forward with her gray hair bloody.

Magda stood and turned and vomited on the floor.

But Alice!

God in heaven, have mercy on us, have mercy on us.

She had to get back.

For Alice.

• • •

The pony's hoofs thundered down, cracking twigs, sliding on snowy leaves and clattering on rocks.

Alice.

She had no time to think, or think properly, and everything was like a mist in front of her eyes. The day had not yet broken fully and the sky was still low with clouds that threatened more snow.

On the pony galloped and she was ill with it and thought that maybe she would do herself some terrible damage but then the damage was already done and she had to get the girl. *God help you if they have come into Gourty's house already*, and the trees flashed past in the darkness and suddenly she was out on the field beside the stream, her breath so hard and her body moving in ways that were not good and her face wet.

Up above the shadow of the farm she pulled the sweating pony to a stop.

Coming from behind the thin line of trees, down in the dip where the Dolgellau road ran, there was a rumbling.

The heavy sound of an engine that drew nearer, but there were no lights. Then she saw something moving down by the road.

A truck pulled up from the lane. She saw its square snout nosing out from the hedge. Another vehicle rumbling somewhere near.

How long before they came up like an ill wind to Gourty's house, looking there for things to steal?

She pushed the pony on. Up through the trees on the slope. Soon she had come close behind the house, could see the mound of the manure heap, could smell it.

A snowflake fell, and then another.

She slid down and tied the pony to a tree, leaned against its flank, her body beating strange rhythms, churning, her breathing so hard and fast and things moving within her.

Not now. Please. Not yet.

Stumbling down the bank, she came to the back of the house, to the woodshed, with the barrows leaning against the wall, and she crept with her breath so loud and fast, and her head seething.

The barnyard was quiet. She dipped along the house under the windows and slipped into the porch. She opened the latch.

Heart thumping, she crossed the floor of the kitchen, the blood drained from her hands and feet and concentrated in her guts with the adrenaline almost bursting from her throat.

Please God, the key is still in your pocket.

It was, and she turned it in the lock.

Up the creaking stairs.

Into the bedroom so dark.

Push aside the clothes and crouch down to find Alice still there, asleep. Mercy.

Alice opened her eyes, blinking.

"Is the game over now?"

"Alice. The game is not over yet. The game is only just beginning. We have to leave the house and be so quiet that not even the mice can hear us. And then we will have to ride in the dark. We must go now."

"Why?"

"Shh. No talking, remember." She took the child by the hand and together they came down the stairs.

The front door was open as she had left it. They crept over the stones and came out into the farmyard. There was a little more light in the sky, but only just, and the snow was falling heavy again.

Alice was heavy in her arms as she carried her now, and she heard voices.

Close. Maybe back behind the barn. Someone had come. She slunk into the shadows as two rangy Liverpool slaughter-men came stealthy and ratlike into the yard with heavy sticks in their hands.

But Magda was up behind the manure heap and into the darkness of the trees where she had left the pony.

The slope was steep and she struggled with the little girl's weight. The pony let out a sharp whinny when he smelled the adrenaline on her.

The little stallion stamped his feet, tugging his head up against the rein. Magda lifted Alice onto his back—high up at the withers where the mane was short and stiff. She stuck her heel into the crook of a coppiced hazel because there was no saddle, no stirrup with which to haul herself up. She tried to pull the pony close, grabbing at its tail even to bring it broadside enough for her to mount.

The young stallion kicked out at such injustice. She slipped from the crook in the tree. Alice lurched, but grabbed the wiry mane and did not fall.

Now there were the sounds of voices loud.

"There's another one up here somewhere!"

Torchlight flickering from around the back of the house, wavering up through the trees.

"Magda—" Alice whimpered, sensing now that this was far from a game.

Magda put her heel back in the hazel crook and pulled the

pony alongside, throwing herself up onto his back as he passed with an impatient skittering step—and she was on, her arms reaching around Alice to grasp at the reins. She hung, unbalanced, for several moments. The pony turned toward the farm, which is where he wanted to go. And she righted herself at last. Hauled him by the mouth. Up. Away into the forest.

There were footsteps in the darkness behind. Shouts, twigs snapping, torchlight dancing among the trunks.

She kicked with all her might at the poor young stallion's sides and he jumped forward and hastened away into the deep trees. How perilous it was to go so fast.

But no matter, and Alice safe between her arms as they headed wide into the woods with pounding hoofbeats under them. Into the woods that stretched around for miles and miles and miles. Into the tangled forest of Coed-y-Brenin, where Magda had never been before.

And the spirit of the forest, Lesh ee, bent down with woody fin gers and he looked at the girl, lost with her foolish dream of Crow.

He saw that her boots were indeed upon the wrong foot and that her clothes were inside out and he whispered with his barky voice through his frosted beard and the breath curled up like mist.

"Crow Alone: there is no Mountain of Glass, nor any houses built from gingerbread, nor princes lost for you to save. There is just this endless forest and, I tell you, that is all you need to understand."

And he prodded at her with his great finger and she awoke at last.

35

The very first traces of daylight tinged the last silver-brown leaves still clinging to the baring branches. It was cold, with the fresh metallic smell of snow in the air, and the pony too was frightened so far from home. It flung its head up at any noise with ears pricked forward. Magda did not know which direction she should take. So she let it find its own way, for it certainly was going somewhere.

Alice, so exhausted, bumped against Magda's encircling arms. And Magda felt that it was happening now. Ivan was with her. The two halves of him. Two beating hearts. But it would not be real until it was out.

She was very afraid. There was fear on every side of her. Behind and beside. Within and without.

The pain was coming in waves now, unbearable pain that she had not imagined. She let out great cries and could bear no longer to be up on the pony.

The pain washed over her and filled every last inch of her head. There was nowhere left for the pain to go except out in her cries, and she dropped the reins, one hand holding her hard, swollen stomach.

The baby is coming.

"Alice. We have to stop."

And Alice said, "Can we go home now?"

The contractions came again.

"Get off, Alice!"

Alice did not know what to make of this new, hard voice. She began to cry. Magda grabbed the little arm and pulled Alice off the pony, dangling her roughly onto the ground, and then she fell forward on the pony's neck, contorted with another spasm. She grabbed the mane and let herself slide down to the earth and turned and fell on her hands and knees in the frosted bracken at the side of the path.

"What's wrong?" Alice cried.

"The baby's coming, Alice. Tie the pony up."

She was so thirsty, and tired. Wanted to close her eyes and rest. But the pains would not let her.

In the recess of her consciousness, she could hear the trickling of water.

"Alice, find some water. I can—hear it."

"I'm scared—"

Magda raised her head and saw that Alice was frightened by her. "Come here." She stroked the girl's face. "I'm sorry. It is very painful, Alice. Please try and find some water for me."

Alice did what she was told. She left the path. The trees were thick with twiggy branches. Her young eyes darted from tree trunk to tree trunk.

Alice, don't go too far.

She could hear Magda calling, back from the path. Down on

the banks of a hollow, a small spring gushed from the rocks, melting the snow where it pooled.

And then she saw the fence. High, but made from wire and pine branches with dead brown needles and bits of wood and metal all green and gray and foreboding.

And behind it, down in the dank hollow among the trees, was a house. The house was mean-looking: boarded at every window, with a patched roof, and piles of logs, and a long, low animal shed. The ground around the house was turned to earth with the last of the kale sticking up in neat rows. By the walls were all sorts of bits of metal junk. Smoke drifted out of the chimney, thin and acrid. And Alice came slipping down the bank and some other creature whinnied from the long, low shed and a dog barked and she ran toward the house without any fear.

"She needs water!" she called loudly.

A dog barked again.

There was a pulling back of bolts.

A tall man with reddish hair appeared at the door with a gun in his hands.

We have seen him before, caught glimpses of him hiding at the dark edges of the forest.

But when he saw the child out on the snow he laid the gun against the wall and came running across the patch of ground and unlocked his gate. He heard what the child said then followed her footprints in the snow. When he pushed aside the branches at the edge of the path, he recognized Callum Gourty's young stallion. There was a woman too, wild in pain but frightened seeing him standing there. He saw too that the little girl was right about what was coming.

"Who are you?" the man said, crouching down.

"Magda. From Rathged Farm."

He helped her up. "What happened?"

"Men came. Killed Bran and Anwen. And the dog. I saw the blood—"

"And Callum. What about Callum Gourty?"

"Gone to Barmouth." Magda doubled over again. "With Bethan."

"It has started then," said the man almost to himself. But he did not mean Magda. She looked up, grasping her belly. "Come on." He looped her arm over his shoulder. "You're safe now. It isn't far."

• • •

The man brought Magda into his warm, dark house. There was just one candle burning on a table. Alice watched silently. He helped Magda up the stairs to a low-ceilinged room where there was a bed.

She let out more cries. So he went immediately to the kitchen. He poured water from the kettle into a wide tin bowl, took a knife, and came back up the stairs.

He took up a position at the end of the bed and without a word he prepared what he thought he must prepare because he had done this before.

"Will it be all right?" Magda gasped.

"Don't worry," the man said. He handed her a cup of water. "I've done it before. You've come far enough. You've got to push now."

She stared with wide-open eyes and gulped at the water.

The man looked at her straight.

"Just push."

The door creaked open. And the small boy came into the room.

"Keep out," said the man without looking over his shoulder. "Get the girl to the fire and pour her some milk and neither of you bother me until I say. You hear me?"

The little boy went downstairs and did as he was told. Alice drank from her mug of milk. The little boy stared at her as the shouts came muffled through the floorboards.

"Are you gonna be my sister?"

Alice glanced over her milk at him.

This time there was a tiny cry from the room above.

The children looked up.

And then another.

After some time there were heavy footfalls on the stairs and they heard the man open the front door and throw the bowl of bloody water out onto the snow.

He came back into the kitchen and looked at the children.

"You can go up if you like. There are two babies. You won't see that again, I reckon." He went to the stove and poured some milk into a pan and heated it gently.

"It's winter now, isn't it?" Alice said. "All the snow."

"Yes. But the summer will come again."

She stared at him. "Can I go home?"

He didn't answer.

"Is Magda died?"

"No."

"Are the babies from her tummy died?"

He lifted Alice from the floor and carried her up to the small room. The stairs were narrow and crooked and he came onto the small landing before the low wooden door.

The man lifted the latch and pushed it open. The little boy had come up too and looked sheepish from behind his father's legs.

"See," said the man, putting Alice down on the floor. "They are just sleeping. Twins."

And they were, two tiny sleeping babies at Magda's breast. Life that had fallen to earth. Resting there. *The half that Ivan had left.*

Alice tottered across the floor and peered up over the mattress. "What are their names?"

"I'm not sure yet," said Magda. "You'll have to help me think of some, won't you?"

Sucking at her fingers, Alice climbed up onto the covers of the bed, and from that place of safety she looked at the strange boy and the man standing tall by the door.

"I'm Robin Blake," said the man. He grasped the boy's thin shoulders and pushed him forward.

"And this is my boy. Willo."

Robin Blake. Magda looked at them standing there. This was the man she had seen leading his pony through the trees. The man who had left the hareskins. The man Callum Gourty had talked about. *"He's likable enough and, even if he doesn't say much, when he does it's worth hearing . . . Likes to keep himself to himself—"*

300

Callum Gourty had been here before.

And there was no strange smell to the house.

She noticed that now. No strange smell at all. Something she thought she knew.

Something like home.

Mary was quiet. She could see the wind-whipped sea casting frothing gray fingers up and out over the black rocks down on the beach below.

Up and out like it always did, and it always had done, and it always would.

Willo got up and put his arm around her shoulders—which was rare enough—and she leaned into it. "I haven't got a heart for much more," she whispered.

"Well, the baby's sleeping," Willo said. "All anyone needs is a bit of rope to cling to."

Mary looked up at the side of his face and saw his eyes were glassy. "I didn't get it all right—about your da and everything. Or Magda. I know I had to make some bits up."

"Don't matter. It was a good Tell. We haven't got anything except old stories for remembering things by, and things ain't turned out too bad either. Always need some kind of happy ending. You done it well. Cos we know Magda been happy enough with my dad in the end."

The baby fluttered its hand.

"You really think so?"

"Yes, Mary," Willo said. "I really do."

And Crow, who had watched and waited and pried at keyholes all this time, shuffled its wings and moved about its roost and, closing its eyes, Crow went to sleep at last.

It was
After all
Only a crow.

Thanks to:

Natalia Valentinovna Generalova, for her uncompromising stance
on life;

Julia Churchill, my agent;

Emma Young, my editor;

Tim, for patience;

Gordon, for his critical eye;

and Lauren Ace and Teleri Dyer for the Welsh translation.

Macmillan UK wishes to thank Liz Cope.